the HANNAH WEST SERIES,

by LINDA JOHNS:

Book 1, *Hannah West in the Belltown Towers*:

"Johns has concocted a wonderful character in twelve-year-old Hannah West, who wanders the street, closely observing her surroundings. Adopted from China as an infant, Hannah and her adoptive mother, an artist, earn their way by house-sitting, with Hannah making extra money as a dog walker and errand runner. [A] great backstory and an engaging heroine . . ."   —*Booklist*

"[A] delightful mystery."   —*Children's Literature*

Book 2, *Hannah West in Deep Water*:

"Hannah is inquisitive, lively, and outspoken, and her often-droll first-person narrative incorporates plenty of local flavor, as well as a growing awareness of marine conservation issues."   —*Booklist*

"Linda Johns creates a convincing setting with plenty of detail about her hometown. Hannah is an appealing protagonist, who unravels the mystery efficiently, but with enough bumps along the way to be satisfying. This is fiction that is both fun and educational."

—*Children's Literature*

Book 3, *Hannah West in the Center of the Universe*: Selected as a **Global Reading Challenge Book**.

Book 4, *Hannah West on Millionaire's Row*:
"There is something irresistible about a young, precocious sleuth. Hannah West is no exception, adding a modern Northwestern twist to the age-old formula. [F]ans will like Hannah's breezy tone and upbeat personality, and they'll appreciate her love of dogs and books, and the copious details she offers about life in Seattle . . . [G]irls looking for a brainy, modern-day Trixie Belden will find Hannah West a contender."

—*Booklist*

NANCY PEARL
PRESENTS
A BOOK CRUSH REDISCOVERY

HANNAH WEST

SLEUTH on the TRAIL

By Linda Johns

two lions

With gratitude to Nancy Pearl and Nancy Johns Heard

two lions

This is a work of fiction. Names, characters, organizations, places, events, and incidents are either products of the author's imagination or are used fictitiously.

Text copyright © 2007 Linda Johns
Introduction copyright © 2016 Nancy Pearl

Published by Two Lions, New York

www.apub.com

Amazon, the Amazon logo, and Two Lions are trademarks of Amazon.com, Inc., or its affiliates.

This book was originally published as two volumes,
Hannah West in the Center of the Universe and *Hannah West on Millionaire's Row*.

ISBN-13: 9781503947177 (hardcover)
ISBN-10: 1503947173 (hardcover)
ISBN-13: 9781503946828 (paperback)
ISBN-10: 1503946827 (paperback)

Cover art © 2016 Michael S. Heath
Book design by Virginia Pope

Printed in The United States of America

CONTENTS

INTRODUCTION

When I was a kid I read the first thirty-four Nancy Drew mysteries, in order, from *The Secret of the Old Clock* to *The Hidden Window Mystery*. Truth be told, I am not sure now, looking back, why I kept reading them. I had no desire at all to be a detective, and didn't much identify with Nancy and her chums. At the same time I also read the first thirteen novels in the Dana Girls series, also by Carolyn Keene, the author of the Nancy Drew mysteries, as well as every other mystery that I could find, including the long-running series starring Frank and Joe Hardy.

My love for mysteries has continued unabated throughout my life, and I am always on the lookout for new ones to read, whether they're aimed at adults, teens, or children. When I moved to Seattle, children's librarians and booksellers kept telling me how much kids enjoyed the four mysteries featuring a twelve-year-old Chinese-American detective named Hannah West. And once I read them I could see why. Hannah is smart, brave, and resourceful; the mysteries she solves are both complex and interesting. Starting with *Hannah West in the Belltown Towers*, these are perfect for eight- to twelve-year-olds who love realistic fiction.

I was thrilled to have the opportunity to interview Linda Johns about writing the Hannah West novels on page 271.

—Nancy Pearl

BOOK ONE

HANNAH WEST
in the
CENTER
of the
UNIVERSE

CHAPTER 1

"I HAVE A surprise for you in the car," Mom said.

One could only hope it was a maple bar and a frosty blue Gatorade.

Practice was supposed to last just ninety minutes this morning, but we played more than two hours, and I was thirsty. I hadn't even noticed the time. That's just the way it is when I'm playing ultimate Frisbee. I'm still on the B team (you can probably guess that the A team is the best) for Cesar Chavez Middle School, but I'm getting a lot of play time this year.

Mom clicked the remote on her key chain to unlock the doors of our old Honda. The car chirped as it unlocked, simultaneously triggering something to pop up in the front passenger seat.

"Elvis!" I cried. I hurried to the car and opened the door, steadying myself as fifty-two pounds of hound came hurling toward me, covering me with slobbery kisses hello. "I'm so happy to see you!" I said, and I meant it. I find it's absolutely, positively impossible to be in a bad mood when there's a funny-looking basset hound around.

"Watch this," Mom said. "Elvis, backseat," she commanded. His long, wiggly body did a 180-degree turn and obediently went into the backseat, turning another 180 degrees until he was facing the front of the car. "Good boy. Now, sit," Mom instructed him. Elvis put his bottom on the backseat and leaned his front paws on the cup holder between the front seats.

"At least half of him is in the backseat," I said, buckling my seatbelt. "How come you already have the dog with you?"

"I dropped Piper off at the airport, and it seemed like it might be less stressful to Elvis if he didn't think he was being abandoned in the apartment. Piper says he gets a little woeful when she starts packing," Mom said.

I turned to look at the basset's droopy brown eyes and wrinkly face. "Doesn't he always look woeful?" I asked. As if responding to my rhetorical question, Elvis rested his chin on my shoulder and let out a sigh.

Elvis's owner, Piper Christensen, had hired Mom and me to stay in her apartment and take care of everything—including her dog—while she was in Hong Kong for an eight-week business trip.

You can look at Mom's and my life one of two ways: either we're homeless or we're professional house sitters. I prefer to see our situation in professional house-sitting terms. The past year has been one house-sitting job after another, so we always had a roof over our heads. Lots of times, including this assignment, we've had some pretty nice roofs over our heads.

We headed down the hill from Bobby Morris Playfield, where I had just finished my marathon ultimate Frisbee session. Mom turned right on Sixth Avenue in downtown Seattle and headed north until we got to Lake Union and the Wooden Boat Center. I checked the street sign: Westlake. Out of habit I checked bus stops and bus numbers along the way: 16, 26, 28. It looked like those all headed toward our new home. We went past the group of houseboats where an old 1990s movie, *Sleepless in Seattle*, was filmed. I could see the Fremont Bridge ahead of us.

"There should be a law that more bridges are painted happy colors," I said, taking in the vivid orange and blue of the drawbridge that headed over the canal, connecting Queen Anne Hill and Seattle's Fremont neighborhood. As it turned out we had lots of time to enjoy the colors up close. Lights on the bridge started blinking, bells started ringing, and a metal barrier came down to stop cars from crossing the bridge. Mom turned off the engine, and we hopped out. Most people stay in their cars and wait, usually impatiently, for the bridge to lower so that traffic can start moving again. But unless it's pouring buckets of rain, Mom and I always get out to watch the action. This time a supertall sailboat motored through.

"We'll probably be seeing this a lot," Mom said. "I heard that the bridge opens frequently."

"Approximately thirty-five times a day, making it one of the busiest drawbridges in the United States," I rattled off. In addition to checking out Metro bus schedules, I always research the history of whatever new neighborhood we are staying in—however temporary it might be.

The bridge deck lowered, car engines started, and traffic began moving both ways across the bridge.

When our car reached the other side, Mom turned to me with a grand gesture and said, "Welcome to the Center of the Universe."

"Huh?"

CHAPTER 2

"I THOUGHT YOU researched all of this," Mom said.

"D'oh!" I said. How could I forget? The Fremont neighborhood had dubbed itself the Center of the Universe. According to my research on Wikipedia, residents of this area of Seattle, about three miles north of downtown, referred to their neighborhood either as the People's Republic of Fremont or as the Center of the Universe. I wasn't exactly sure why, except that Fremont had gone from a hippie haven to a high-priced neighborhood with trendy restaurants.

"Darn it, I'm in the wrong lane to turn. I'm going to have to go around the block," Mom said. The extra drive was okay with me. I liked looking at the restaurants and shops, and this way we'd get to go right by one of Seattle's most famous statues.

"Go slow here! I want to see what the people are wearing today," I said to Mom. We were right next to this cast-aluminum sculpture of six life-sized figures—including a little dog—huddled together as if they were waiting for a bus or a train or something. It's officially called *Waiting for the Interurban*, so I guess they're supposed to be waiting for the train. They don't exactly look happy, but I guess I wouldn't be either if I'd been waiting a few decades for a train that never comes. The thing I like best is that people put costumes on the bus people statues. According to Wikipedia, this is usually done in the middle of the night so that in the morning they have fresh outfits, hats, balloons, signs, and even umbrellas if there's a chance of rain and scarves around their necks when it's cold. Kind of like dressing a permanent snowman.

Today must have been Western theme day. The metal people wore cowboy hats and bandannas. A large sign said, "Happy Birthday, Trixie!" The little dog had a blue bandanna tied around his neck and a party hat on his head. Someone had taped a yellow sign to the dog's tail. The traffic light turned green and we started moving, so I couldn't read what the yellow sign said.

We soon came to a very tall building, and I realized I was looking at the Epi. That's the name of the apartment building where we were going to live. It's actually called the Epicenter, as in the Center of the Center of the Universe, but Piper told us people just call it "the Epi." Purple and blue served as a backdrop for metal swirls on the outside of the six-story building. It was whimsical and fun, proving that not all adults take themselves too seriously. I loved it. Seriously loved it.

"How totally cool is this?" I asked as Mom turned into the

alley and into the parking garage below a big supermarket. "I'm so excited to live above a grocery store. Snickers bars just an elevator ride away."

"I wouldn't count on that," Mom said, laughing. Elvis added a bark. "I'll take him, so you can take these two." She handed me my goldfish, Vincent and Pollock. They were inside a Ziploc bag that I'd placed inside their glass bowl so the water wouldn't slosh out.

Mom and I have this ritual about moving into a new place: we always save our most precious belongings for the final load. Luckily for me, Mom and her friend Nina had moved most of our stuff to Piper's apartment earlier in the day while I was at ultimate Frisbee. I really had only one trip to make upstairs to carry my current sketchbook, backup sketchbooks (one can never have too many), and some photos in my messenger bag. I picked up a painting I did at art camp and the bowl with my fish.

We'd be able to go straight from underground parking garage to fourth-floor apartment via elevator. But the elevator stopped on the lobby floor.

"Hold the elevator, please," a man called. He was pinning a bright yellow flyer to the bulletin board in the lobby. I could see the word "Missing" in big letters. It looked like the same sign I'd seen taped to the dog statue.

"Thanks," he said as he got on the elevator. Elvis tried to sniff his pockets. "Sorry, but I don't have anything for you, Elvis," he said.

"So you know Elvis?" Mom said. "We'll be taking care of him and Piper's apartment for the next two months. My name is Maggie West, and this is my daughter, Hannah West."

He looked at both of us. He didn't look happy. Not mad. Just sort of sad. Maybe preoccupied.

I moved my fingers in an attempt to wave without dropping my goldfish.

The man nodded. I noticed he wasn't offering up his name or any details. He took a roll of tape from his coat pocket and started taping the corner of a yellow flyer to the elevator wall. The stack of papers he'd been carrying scattered on the floor just as we got to the fourth floor and the elevator doors opened.

"Let me help you," I said. Mom pushed the button to keep the elevator door open while I put down my belongings and knelt to pick up papers.

"Oh, no! Is it your dog that's lost?" I said, finally getting a good look at the yellow flyer that said "Missing."

"He's not lost. He's missing. Boris disappeared earlier today," he said dejectedly, handing a flyer to me as we headed into the hallway.

A blurry photo of a dog was centered at the top of the page. Below its picture it said:

```
         Missing!

    Please help find
         Boris,
    a two-year-old
      bichon frise.

       Disappeared
   Saturday morning.
      Last seen on
  the sidewalk outside
    Joe's Special.

       Reward!!!
```

"Do you think he was stolen? Snatched? Maybe even dognapped?" I asked. Mom gave me that stern parent look that usually means, in my case, "Stop jumping to conclusions."

"That's exactly what I think," the man said. "One second he was there. The next he was gone. Vanished. Vamoosed. I'm Ted, by the way. I live three doors down from Piper. She made sure everyone on this floor knew that you two were coming to house-sit and take care of Elvis."

"We appreciate that," Mom said. "Let us know what we can do to help find your dog." I knew Mom was sincere, but it sounded like one of those things people automatically say when they don't think they can possibly help.

"I can definitely help track him down," I said.

I fished a business card out of my pocket and handed it to Ted.

Hannah J. West

Pet Sitter, Dog Walker,
Plant Waterer, and
all around Errand Girl

235-6628

Ted gave me a slight smile, but I don't think he took my offer seriously. He had other things on his mind.

But I already had an idea about what I could do to help.

CHAPTER 3

"I HAVE TO call Lily," I said, practically mowing Mom over in the entryway to apartment 409 and running down the hall to the kitchen. I'd been to Piper's apartment twice before to meet Elvis, so I knew exactly where to go. I needed to get to a water source and my cell phone. When you move around as much as we do, you cling to whatever rituals and traditions you have. One of mine was to call Lily within seconds of moving to our new pad. The other one was to get Vincent and Pollock into their bowl as soon as possible. Mom disappeared farther down the hallway to the living room to call her friend Nina.

In a total show of ambidexterity, I used my left hand to dial Lily's phone number and my right hand to pour Vincent and Pollock into their bowl.

"Lily! It's me. I'm at the new apartment, and I think I may have already found my next case," I said, wiping up the water I'd spilled all over the kitchen counter. Apparently I'd overestimated my ambidextrous abilities.

"A new case? I haven't dried off from our last one," she

said. "Does this one include television appearances?"

"Um, excuse me. Who needs TV when we've got real-life action?" Here we were, typical middle schoolers by day and cunning detectives by night, yet Lily was more interested in whether we could talk our way into being extras on a TV show like we were over the summer, on the set of *Dockside Blues*.

"Well, you don't exactly make money in the crime-solving business," she said.

She had a point. We had each made a hundred bucks as extras in that cable TV drama. But our brush with fame also put us in the middle of a mystery. Which we'd solved, of course.

"This case has a significant reward," I said, trying to entice her.

"Okay, you've got my attention now," she said.

"A dog is missing from our new apartment building," I said. "There are signs all over the neighborhood about it."

Silence on the other end of the phone. Then, a big sigh. "Hannah, a missing dog is hardly a crime. Granted, it's heartbreaking, but the pooch could be seeking kibble elsewhere. A lost dog does not indicate criminal activity."

Now it was my turn to sigh. Lily, of all people, should know to trust my intuition on these things. "It might not officially be a dognapping—yet. I still want to do some digging around. Did I mention there's a reward?"

"I'm sure I can convince my dad to give me a ride over

there. He's all excited about you and Maggie living on top of one of the Puget Sound Co-op Natural Markets, better known in our house as PCC," she said.

"Great," I said. "I'll see you soon." I tried to hide the disappointment in my voice. It's not that I wasn't excited to see Lily—I was. After all, she was my best friend. It was the fact that her dad was excited about PCC Natural Market that was bumming me out. I've learned from experience that the kinds of markets that get Dan Shannon excited are not the kinds of supermarkets that carry Snickers bars.

While I waited for Lily to arrive, I looked around for the best place to put Vincent and Pollock's fishbowl so it would be safe from the dog. Elvis might have short legs, but Piper had warned us that his long body makes it so he can "counter surf," rise up on his back legs and reach the kitchen counters. He does it in search of food, but I didn't want to take any chances.

"Whoa!" I said, carrying the fishbowl into the living room. When I'd visited the apartment before it had been nighttime. I could tell there was a view, but I had no idea that the corner windows would have such a spectacular view of the canal. Those metal swirls that decorated the outside of the building actually overlapped part of the windows, almost as if punctuating the view. I put my fish on top of a small hutch and headed back down the hall. I pushed the two doors that were ajar all the way open, and was thrilled to see that they were both bedrooms. One was obviously Piper's—my mom would use that one. So I checked out the other one.

"Whoa!" I said again. No one had told me I was going to have my own bathroom and a walk-in closet. I bopped across the hall to check out Mom's bedroom, which also had a bathroom and walk-in closet. "My" bedroom, however, had two added bonuses: a TV and a velvet-covered chaise longue for my TV-watching comfort. "This place seems almost as big as our old house," I said a bit wistfully. I missed having a real home that we could call our own.

"Actually it's a bit bigger than our old house. About two hundred square feet bigger," Mom said.

I unpacked my clothes and hung them in the walk-in closet. They took up about one-hundredth of the closet space. I arranged my books, sketchbooks, CDs, and photos on the bookshelves. I guess the good thing about having sold most of our possessions is that unpacking takes only about nine minutes.

I was checking out the television channels at my disposal (at least ninety) when Lily buzzed. "Quick, let me up!" she said frantically over the intercom. "My dad is threatening to drag me into the grocery store and give me a tour of the produce aisle and tell me which vegetables are the highest source of vitamin K or Q or whatever."

I buzzed her in and told her how to get to our new apartment. I know it's not really "our" apartment, but it's too clunky to say "the apartment where we're house-sitting" or even "Piper's apartment."

When she got up to the apartment, I gave Lily the grand tour, leading her down the hallway and showing off the bedrooms and the bright kitchen. I saved the view for last. "Whoa," Lily exclaimed, echoing my earlier amazement. I had to admit, it was an impressive view.

We headed back into "my" bedroom, and I showed Lily the bright yellow flyer.

"Look! See how there are three exclamation points after the word reward?" I asked.

"The overuse of exclamation points, in addition to being irritating, is usually done by those who are trying to make something out of nothing," Lily said. "In this case, I bet it means a teensy tiny reward for a teensy tiny dog."

I pulled out my copy of *Legacy of the Dog*, a book about dog breeds that I've practically memorized. I quickly turned to the toy group section and found a two-page spread on the bichon frise. "Meet the bee-shahn free-zay, so much more than what you call a teensy-tiny chien," I said, trying to sound French to pique Lily's interest. But I knew once Lily saw photos of this little white fluffy dog she'd be hooked, with or without my lame attempt at an accent.

"Oh, look," she practically cooed. "Its name means 'curly-haired puppy.' We have to help find this little fluff ball." We read about the bichon frise together, learning that it was only about ten inches tall, weighed only about ten pounds, and has been around since the Middle Ages. The book also noted that the breed has a "pretentious gait," which I think could also be interpreted as the dog has a happy, jaunty walk. My preschool teacher at Montessori Garden had a dog like this named Bijoux, and it was about the sweetest dog I've ever met.

"It sounds like the perfect dog. Ack!" Lily squealed as she looked down. "And speaking of dogs, you must be Elvis."

Piper's basset hound was licking Lily's wrist, an act of sincere friendliness that Lily seemed unable to fully appreciate.

"Come here, Elvis," I said, and immediately the hound transferred his licking to me. "Look at these ears! How could you not love these velvety soft ears?" I asked, petting Elvis's eight-inch-long brown ears.

"And look at all this extra skin," Lily said, grabbing hunks of skin around his neck. "He looks like old, fat Elvis Presley from the 1970s, not young, cute Elvis from the 1950s. Eww! He stinks, too."

"He doesn't stink. He just has a distinctive houndy odor. He also has a magnificent nose, second only to a bloodhound in terms of its power. And, I might add, he's of French descent."

"Uh-huh. He still stinks," Lily said.

I have to admit Elvis did smell kind of doggy. It's a good thing basset hounds are so cute. Their long bodies, short legs, sad faces, and soulful eyes make them pretty irresistible. I could tell he was winning Lily's devotion. She started singing "You ain't nothing but a hound dog" in a twisted attempt to sound like Elvis Presley.

"Maybe Elvis will be my new sidekick. He can track Boris. You know, Columbo had a basset," I said. I love old 1970s and 1980s detective TV shows, and one of my favorites is *Columbo*, where this seemingly absent-minded detective in a trench coat brilliantly solved cases in an understated way.

"I hate to tell you that you're not Columbo. You're not even Sherlock Holmes. And Elvis is no hound of the Baskervilles," Lily said. We recently read *The Hound of the Baskervilles* in Language Arts. The horrific hound causing centuries of havoc in that story was nothing like the sweet basset hound lying next to me.

I know that I'm no Sherlock. But I believed that there was something going on behind Boris's disappearance.

I have a nose for these things.

Elvis rubbed his cold nose against my arm, as if he agreed.

CHAPTER 4

ELVIS NUDGED MY arm harder, and I realized that he may not have been agreeing with me as much as he was trying to tell me he needed to go outside.

"Perfect!" Mom said, as I walked into the living room to get Elvis's leash. "Lily, Hannah, get your coats. We'll check out the neighborhood together, with Elvis as a tour guide."

Elvis was ready to lead us, practically pulling us out of the building, through the alley, and up a short flight of stairs that led to Fremont Avenue. Mom was the real tour guide, though, making sure that I knew cross streets and landmarks. Let me tell you, Fremont has some great landmarks. We were walking down Thirty-fifth, and all of a sudden there was this fifty-foot silver rocket on the corner. Across the street was Norm's, a restaurant that lets you bring dogs inside. We peeked inside just to make sure it really would be okay to come back with our dog.

"Well-behaved dogs are always welcome here, as long as the humans are well behaved, too," a man behind the bar said.

As we left Norm's, someone called out, "Elvis has left the building." Apparently everyone really does know Elvis around here.

We kept going, looking at the sights. Besides the bus people statue, there's a tall bronze statue of Vladimir Lenin on a patio outside of a Mexican restaurant. I don't even really know who Lenin was, but according to the sign next to the statue he had been a communist leader of the Soviet Union.

We walked along slowly, allowing Elvis to sniff at whatever he liked while we checked out the windows of a couple of clothing stores and Fremont Place Books. We peeked in at Frank and Dunya, a store that sold pieces by local artists and that had sculpted dogs—named Frank and Dunya, the owner's former dogs—ready to greet us. Mom wasn't kidding when she said that people in Fremont really loved their dogs.

Close to the canal was Costas Opa, a Greek restaurant we go to at least once a year when my mom's cousin is in town. We walked along the canal a little bit, and then we went into Capers, the housewares and home-furnishings store where Mom's friend Polly Summers works. She's the one who set up this house-sitting and dog-sitting gig for us.

"Believe me, you'll need some of this," Polly said, showing us these candles and fragrance sprays called Fresh Wave. "Piper buys this stuff all the time to cover up those houndy smells. No offense, Elvis."

Finally we came to the spot I wanted to visit. Joe's Special. "Hey," I said. "This is the place where Boris was snatched." I started to look around, to see if I could spot any evidence.

"We don't know that the dog was snatched, Hannah," Mom said, with just a bit of warning in her voice.

Ted's yellow "missing" flyers were posted on both windows of the restaurant. Elvis started sniffing around. "Look! He's sniffing for clues! Maybe he's going to track Boris," I said.

"Or maybe he found a piece of bread," Lily added, as Elvis hoovered up a snack and followed his tasty treat with a fit of barking. A *long* fit of barking.

"Shhh!" I tried.

"Quiet!" Mom said.

"Hush!" Lily said.

"Try 'quiet, please,'" said another voice. Elvis stopped barking. Immediately. The first thing I saw was a huge sheepdoglike dog, but at the end of the dog's leash was a guy, maybe around our age. But you can never really tell with boys. In my seventh-grade homeroom, there was a twelve-inch difference between these two guys, Garth and Caleb, who are best friends and have birthdays in the same month.

"I guess that worked," Mom said. "Is that some kind of universal dog command that we don't know?" Mom asked.

"Nah. I just know that Piper uses the phrase 'quiet,

please' in that tone of voice, kind of soft and nice, if you know what I mean. It's the only thing that gets Elvis to stop barking sometimes. If you yell or say something loud, he'll just bark more to try to be heard. Kind of like he's in a contest to outbark you." He looked as if he was sizing us up.

"We're Elvis's dog-sitters, taking care of him for Piper," I said. I didn't want some stranger thinking that we were dognapping Elvis.

"Cool. Piper said to be on the lookout for you guys. This is Scooter. He and Elvis are good pals," the shaggy-dog guy said. The two dogs were sniffing each other happily.

"It's nice to know that people know each other's dogs and are watching out for them," Mom said. "Especially since one of our neighbors just lost his dog."

"I saw the flyer. It doesn't sound like Boris is lost," Shaggy-Dog Guy said. He looked at his watch. "I gotta go. Nice meeting you."

Only we didn't really meet him.

"He never said his name," Lily pointed out. "Then again, we didn't tell him ours either."

"Yeah, but he did say that he thinks Boris was dognapped," I said.

"Hannah!" Lily and Mom said together, which got Elvis barking again.

"Quiet, please," I said nicely to Elvis. It worked. "Okay, he didn't actually say dognapped, but he implied that he thought something was up, too." Elvis was pulling his leash over to a bowl of water labeled "Fresh Dog Water." The window above was painted with the store's name, "The Perfect Pet: Grooming, Treats, Toys."

"Hey, I know that woman," I said, pointing to the woman at the counter inside. "She volunteers at the animal shelter." I waved. She looked right at us but didn't wave back. Maybe the sun was in her eyes or something.

"Um, Maggie, I need to go, too. My dad is picking me up soon. We have to go to this symphony thing tonight. My parents have decided we need some culture in our lives," Lily said.

We headed back to our building. Yellow flyers with Boris's photo were in every shop window. Every window except The Perfect Pet, that is.

CHAPTER 5

"HERE YOU GO, Izzie," I said, placing a fresh bowl of water in front of my new best friend the next morning. Mom had dropped me off at the Elliott Bay Animal Shelter on Sunday morning for my weekly volunteer job. "Actually, you're one of my three best friends," I said, scratching behind her ears. "I just worry the most about you."

A beam of sunlight came through the window and lit up a triangle of Izzie's gleaming brown fur. I interpreted this as a sign that things were going to get better for this love muffin of a dog. Izzie looked at me and hesitated, as if making sure it was okay to go to the bowl.

"Go ahead, it's for you," I said. She slurped the water eagerly. An enthusiastic head shaking after her drink sprayed water everywhere. She turned back to me and rested her chin against my thigh. My heart ached to think what kind of a life Izzie must have had. I have a pretty good imagination, but I just couldn't understand how someone could mistreat an animal. "Especially you, Izzie," I said, scratching her behind her right ear. The ray of sunlight was now hitting the exact outline of a white patch of fur on her nose. I decided to take that as an even bigger sign that things were about to get better for this dog.

Izzie and I have a lot in common. We're both technically homeless (I already told you about that), we're both smart (if I do say so myself), and I'm adopted and she's going to be adopted. I used all my positive-thinking energy about her getting adopted, and soon.

Izzie had come to the Elliott Bay Dog Shelter last month. She brought along the equivalent of an entire city of fleas. The poor thing was an itchy, scratchy, miserable mess. Big chunks of fur were missing because she had hot spots, which is what happens when a dog has fleas and is supersensitive to them. I was there the day she arrived. We didn't know much about her at first, except that she was itchy, sensitive (to fleas and in spirit), and timid. By the second week a little more of her personality was showing through, and it was time to photograph her and get an ad up on the Web site to find her a new home. I asked Leonard if I could take a stab at writing her ad. Here's what I wrote:

> *Leggy, svelte, smart, sensitive, and sweet adult female looking for the perfect match. Loves long walks in the woods, taking scenic rides in your car with the windows rolled down, listening to all kinds of music, eating quiet dinners in the kitchen,*

snuggling on the couch, and relaxing by a fire.

Leonard made me take out the "leggy" part because he said it was starting to sound too much like the ads grown-ups use to try to find true love on those Web sites that have words like *harmony* and *love* in their names. That, of course, was the whole point. I'd read in the newspaper about an animal shelter that placed a funny ad like that and got hundreds of calls for a Labrador puppy named Daisy. Of course, I'd also read that the Daisy story was an urban legend. Anyway, if there's one thing I learned in the Cesar Chavez Middle School Writing Workshop, it's that first drafts need to be rewritten. Here's my revision:

Meet Izzie, a smart, sensitive, and sweet adult female dog, approximately five years old. This large mixed-breed (Lab, maybe some rottweiler, and dogs from other diverse backgrounds) has good manners and is eager to please. Knows basic commands and is a fast learner, especially if there's a tasty treat as a reward. Gets along well with the other dogs and cats at the shelter and is gentle with children. Needs regular exercise but is calm and quiet. She has a mysterious past and came to us with fleas, but she's in good health now. Spayed, up-to-date vaccines, and ready for you.

"Nice job, Hannah," Leonard said, even though he still made some edits to the ad. "Working on another sketch of Izzie?"

"She's a good model for me," I said, showing Leonard the latest of the dozen drawings I have of Izzie. I closed my sketchpad and put it back in my messenger bag. "May I take Izzie for another short walk and then help with her bath?"

"Sure. I'll let Meredith know you're bringing Izzie in for a bath and a nail trim. And Hannah," Leonard said, "I know how hard it is to say good-bye to animals, but you have to keep in mind that our job is to find them homes where they'll be safe and loved for the rest of their lives."

I smiled at him, but I still felt like my moist eyes were giving away the fact that I was pretty close to tears. I had been coming to the Elliott Bay Animal Shelter every week for the past couple of months, giving me more than five times as many hours I needed for my community-service requirement at school. Not that community service should even be a requirement. I felt like I should be paying the shelter for the opportunity to be here. In fact, I decided to set aside half of the money I make from dog-walking for the rest of the year and donate it to the shelter.

Fifteen minutes later Izzie and I were back at the shelter and waiting for bath time. A volunteer in the grooming room was finishing up with a huge dog the size of a real-life Scooby-Doo. When she turned around, I realized it was the volunteer who I saw at The Perfect Pet yesterday—Meredith.

"Meredith? Are you ready for us?" I asked tentatively.

"Just finishing up with Cyrano, here," she said. She towel-dried him and clasped a wide collar around his massive neck. I brought a ramp over to the table so that Cyrano could walk down from the grooming table.

"Cyrano is about to go home with a new family," Meredith said. She sighed a long, deep sound that sounded so sad.

"It must be really hard to say good-bye to dogs, even when you know they're going to good homes," I said, paraphrasing what Leonard had just said to me.

"It's not just that," Meredith said, all doom and gloom. "I'd say only five percent of the people who have dogs are worthy of them."

I laughed nervously. She was kidding, right? Oops. I guess not, because she glared at me. I pretended to cough.

"I guess I'm not sure what you mean," I said.

"I don't have any exact figures. No one's ever bothered doing a scientific study on something as important as responsible dog ownership. But I see way too many dogs in my job who are neglected," she said.

"Do you mean your job at The Perfect Pet? I think I saw you there," I said.

She glared at me.

"Did you? Hmmm. Why don't you bring Izzie up here?" she said. I noticed she used a soft, sweet voice to talk to dogs. Her voice to me wasn't nearly as sweet.

Izzie pranced easily up the ramp, but then she seemed a bit scared. Cyrano sat patiently next to me.

"Your new family is here, Cyrano," Leonard said, taking the dog's leash.

"I'm going to miss that big guy," Meredith said. "Do you live in Fremont? With a dog?"

"I'm dog-sitting there," I said. I automatically reached for one of my business cards. I couldn't exactly hand one to Meredith when she was up to her elbows in water and soap.

She raised her eyebrows at me.

"Um, maybe you know him? I'm dog-sitting Elvis. He's a basset hound. A tricolored basset hound," I rattled off quickly. I didn't want to go into the whole thing about house-sitting and everything. Mom and I have to be careful who we tell. We don't want the schools to label me as a transient, because if that happens I won't be able to keep going to Cesar Chavez Middle School with all my friends.

"I think I know him," was all Meredith said.

Okaaaay . . .

"Does Elvis go to The Perfect Pet?" I asked. I don't know why, but the silences in this conversation were making me uncomfortable.

"Don't you know? I would think that a responsible dog sitter would know all of these details," she said. She had a hose in her hand, so I didn't want to say anything that would bug her.

"It sure seems like there are a lot of dogs in Fremont," I said. Why did I keep talking?

"Too many, if you ask me," she said.

That seemed like a weird thing for a dog lover to say.

"I don't know what you mean by that. Is there something wrong with Fremont?" I asked.

"There's nothing wrong with Fremont. It's a great neighborhood," she said. "I'm just not so sure that city dogs get the attention and exercise they need. I'm not convinced that any dog gets the attention and exercise it deserves. Every dog could use more walks."

Izzie's ears perked up at the word *walk*. So did mine. If we were in a cartoon, there'd be a thought bubble above Izzie's head with a person walking her down the street. There would be a thought bubble over my head with a lightbulb and dollar signs inside. I took this opportunity to pull out a business card.

"That's where I can help," I said. "I'm a reliable dog walker with good references."

Meredith took the business card and shoved it into the front pocket of her jeans without even looking at it. Then she looked at me. Intently.

"Keep a close eye on that basset. You wouldn't want anything bad to happen to him." She went back to rinsing Izzie.

What a weird thing to say.

CHAPTER 6

MOM PICKED ME up right after Izzie's bath. I really wanted Izzie to have the best home ever, but my gut ached every time I thought about not seeing her again. I know it's selfish. I tried not to get too emotional. Dogs can pick up on these things, and I wanted Izzie to be confident and happy when prospective new owners came to check her out.

Moms pick up on these emotional things, too. Mine put her arm around my shoulders as we walked to the car. I didn't even pay attention when she pointed the remote control key toward our Honda and clicked "unlock." But I had to smile as Elvis popped up in the front seat. This time I braced myself to stay steady when this drooling hound hurled his body at me.

"I'm never going to forget you, just like I'm never going to forget Izzie," I said, pushing his long wiggly body into the backseat of the car.

"I got the photo from Ted," Mom said. I'd offered to make a crisp black line drawing based on the photo of Boris. Mom thought it was a truly thoughtful idea and had called Ted to ask for a new photo. She handed me a framed picture of Boris, the bichon frise. "The photo on the flyer definitely didn't do him justice."

"I guess this means Boris didn't magically appear while I was at the animal shelter," I said.

Mom's silence was all the answer I needed. I pulled out my sketchbook and started drawing Boris. Drawing in a moving car isn't ideal, but I felt like I needed to do something. If Boris's owner wanted people to be on the lookout for him, it was clear to me that a better picture was needed on the flyer. Sure, the bright yellow paper and the word "Reward!!!" would get people's attention, but the photocopying process had turned Boris's fluffy white head into a muddy, blurry mess.

I kept working on the Boris drawing when we got back to the apartment. I wanted something unique about Boris to come through, but I needed to keep it simple enough so that it would copy well.

By three o'clock, I had it. I scanned the drawing and redesigned Ted's original flyer. Then I printed it on Piper's laser printer. Mom and I took it to Ted's apartment, 403, just down the hall.

"Did you say you're in middle school?" Ted asked. "That's hard to believe because this is so good. You really captured his personality, just from that photograph. It's uncanny." Ted was getting a little choked up. I would choke up, too, if my pet was missing.

"If it's okay with you, I could get this photocopied and we could put them up in the stores and restaurants around the neighborhood. We can go to all the same places where you put the flyer yesterday," I said. Putting up flyers would also give me an excuse to go into all the local shops, maybe even ask people some questions about the last time they saw Boris.

Ted seemed exhausted, and his voice was hoarse—probably from walking up and down the streets calling for Boris. He thanked me and handed me twenty dollars to make copies.

"I was wondering if you could tell me a little more about when he disappeared," I said. "Maybe I might find something because I'll have fresh eyes in the area."

"There's not much to say. He was there one second, gone the next. Boris was patiently waiting for me outside The Perfect Pet while I picked up—"

"The Perfect Pet?" I interrupted. "I thought the flyer said something about Joe's Special."

"I was inside Joe's Special picking up a clubhouse sandwich. I'd called my order in earlier so I wouldn't be inside too long. I tied Boris to a metal post outside The Perfect Pet next door," Ted said.

"How was the leash secured to the post?" I asked, using my best inquiring-detective-wants-to-know voice. Ted grabbed a thin leash from his inside doorknob, looped it around a coatrack, pulled the hook end through the loop, and tightened it. It's the same way I'd secure a leash to a pole or a bench.

"The leash was gone, too," Ted said, confirming my suspicion. There's no way a dog could undo a loop that secure. If a dog had simply run away to follow a squirrel or to find food, the leash would have stayed behind.

"You know, my friends think I'm blowing this all out of proportion," Ted said.

"I don't think you are," I said.

He smiled in that way that says, That's nice of you, kid.

"Did you know that in most dognappings small dogs are taken," I said. I mentioned how the thieves go after small dogs, partly because they're portable but also because they're the hot dogs of the moment. "People pay a lot of money for small purebred dogs, and not all people care where the dogs come from," I said.

Uh-oh. I was getting that warning look from my mom again.

"I'm just sharing what I learned on the Internet . . ." I trailed off.

"I have a feeling you're on the right track," Ted said. "Small dogs are hot, as you say. Bichon frises are known as a highly desirable breed. Hypoallergenic. No shedding. Easy to train. Sweet and loyal."

No one had called to collect on the reward, which makes the dognapping-for-ransom scenario a little weaker. Yet it had been more than twenty-four hours since Boris had disappeared. That seemed to increase the chance that Boris was stolen. The dog thief might have already sold him for a ridiculous amount of money to someone who wanted a cute white dog as a fashion accessory.

"Thanks for all your help," Ted said wearily as Mom and I headed back down the hall. "I'm tempted to have you make one slight change and put the amount of the reward money on it. Perhaps that would help."

I was tempted to ask how much the reward was, but I didn't have to. Ted told me.

No wonder there were three exclamation points after "reward."

CHAPTER 7

"FOUR THOUSAND, two hundred, and fifty *dollars*?" Lily practically screamed into the phone. "That is a huge amount of money."

"Exactly," I said.

"If someone knew that Ted would offer that kind of money, why didn't the dog thief just pretend to find the dog and collect the money?"

"Exactly," I said again.

"Suddenly this case is much more interesting."

"So now you agree that we have a case?" I asked.

I didn't quite catch what Lily said next. She was calling me on her mom's cell phone while they were driving from the Maple Leaf section of Seattle (my old neighborhood) to Fremont. Lily's dad, Dan, wanted to pick up some more organic vegetables at PCC. I'm not sure if the Shannons really needed to come to PCC, but they always go out of their way to make sure Lily and I can spend lots of time together. It takes considerable more coordination now than it did when we lived down the street from each other, and I appreciated the effort.

It wasn't the money that made the case seem more real. Not directly, anyway. It was the fact that the amount of money was so large and still whoever had Boris hadn't tried to collect on it. But then again, people didn't know how big the reward was yet.

"We have to keep the option open that Boris is lost, plain and simple," Lily said. She was in our apartment looking at the flyer.

I gave her a look.

"Yeah, I don't believe it either. But it is still a possibility."

It was already four o'clock on Sunday afternoon. Most stores would close in an hour or two. We needed to get going if we wanted to hang the posters. Also, there was this little thing called homework that I'd successfully put off all weekend. I'd have to find time for that, too.

"Stop fiddling with that thing," Lily said. I was back at my laptop.

"Oh, I'm finished with Ted's flyer. I had another idea."

"Of course you did." Lily sighed.

"Here we go," I said, as Piper's printer spit out another flyer. Lily picked it up. She raised her eyebrows at me. "That's good thinking," she said.

"Let's go get them printed," I said, grabbing Elvis's leash.

"He's coming with us?" Lily asked.

"Of course. He's tracking Boris."

Lily rolled her eyes.

"You have to admit that he gives us an excuse to talk with people," I said. "He's our cover."

When we got to the copy shop, I gave Lily the choice of standing outside with Elvis or going inside to get copies made. Not surprisingly, she chose the inside job.

"Okay, make forty of each of these. Get the one for Boris on that same fluorescent yellow paper and get this other one on bright green."

"Well, hello, young Elvis." An elderly man walking down the street tipped his hat to us. He was the sixth person in five minutes to call Elvis by name. The man stopped and looked at the flyer that said Boris was missing. He made a tsk-tsk sound. "Such a shame, such a shame," he said.

"Here you go," Lily said, coming out with a stack of yellow papers and a stack of green. She pulled the old Boris flyer down.

"Now just a minute, young lady . . . Oh, I see," he said, as he read the new-and-improved flyer. "That is a much better likeness of Boris. You two must be helping Ted out."

This neighborhood was starting to feel like a small town in a movie where everyone knows everyone else's business. You'd think that would make it easier to find a dog. Whoever took Boris would have caught someone's attention. Sure, lots of people come to Fremont to eat and shop, but Boris was a local. They wouldn't just stand around while a stranger walked off with him. Unless the person who took Boris was also a local . . .

"I'm sorry, I didn't hear what you said." I realized that the man in the hat had continued talking while I was mulling things over.

He chuckled. "I was just saying that this is a fine idea," he said, nodding toward my green flyer that Lily had just taped to the window.

Does Your Dog Hate to Shop?

You'll get your errands done faster
if you leave your canine with me.

No more barking outside of shops,
no more worrying about
a tail-wagger breaking something
inside a store.

Call for an experienced
dog walker's help.

References available.

235-6628

I'd illustrated the flyer with cartoon scenes with Elvis, Mango, and Ruff, three of my star clients. Each vignette showed a happy dog walking alongside a responsible-looking twelve-year-old Chinese girl (me).

"Do you have a dog?" I asked.

"Me? No, I don't," he said. He sounded kind of sad. "I love dogs, but I'm afraid my wife was quite allergic. She was fine around cats, but sneezed up a storm around canines. I still have five cats. We had six at one time."

I noticed he talked about his wife and her allergies in the past tense. See? Always thinking. Always gathering information. Maybe this seemingly nice man was a crazy cat person. Maybe he actually hated dogs.

"I'm sorry," I said. I'd missed whatever he'd said. Again. Lily looked at me puzzled. He looked at me puzzled, too.

"I was saying that this is a fine idea, especially given recent events in the neighborhood. I'll be sure to spread the word. If people tell you 'Mack sent me,' you'll know it was me. That's me. I'm Mack." He tipped his hat again. It was one of those old-fashioned bowler hats, the kind that men wore with suits in old movies. His seemed authentic, like he'd had it since the 1950s. "Good day," he said, and moved down the street.

"Nice man. Reminds me of my grandfather," Lily said.

Our next stop was Joe's Special. Lily took another turn inside and I stayed outside with Elvis. I looked at the metal pole outside The Perfect Pet, where Ted had tied Boris's leash. It looked as secure as Ted said. Lily made a face at me through the restaurant window as she taped up our flyers.

"You might as well keep holding him because I'll just pop in here while I'm in the taping mode," she said. She turned the knob to The Perfect Pet, but it was locked. "Weird," she said. The sign was still turned to "Open." According to the hours painted on the door window, they were open another twenty-five minutes. I didn't think it would be polite to tape something to the outside of the shop's windows without their permission. Instead, I slipped two copies of each flyer through the mail slot next to the door.

Our final stop was Peet's Coffee, on the corner of Thirty-fourth and Fremont. I handed the leash to Lily.

"I don't see why we can't both go inside and Elvis can wait for us outside. No offense to the hound, but I don't think anyone would snatch him."

I glared at her.

"I mean, not that he's not adorable and wonderful. But he's rather heavy, so someone can't just pick him up and run. He's also rather vocal, and I think we'd hear about it if someone tried to take him," she said.

I glared at her again.

"What?"

"Ahem! The flyers?" I held up one of the green flyers. "It's completely counterproductive to leave Elvis outside when that's exactly what I'm trying to get people not to do."

"Oh . . . right. Unless you attached the flyers to Elvis's sides, and turned him into a walking outdoor billboard."

That comment didn't warrant a reply. I headed inside the coffee shop to ask if I could replace the "Missing" flyer and put up my green one. I pinned a copy of each on the bulletin board, and then taped two copies on the glass door—one on each side so that people would see them coming and going.

We ran out of flyers quickly. We should have made it to twenty different shops, but several shop owners wanted more than two copies of my green flyer. My friend Polly Summers at Capers, the one who introduced us to Piper, asked for extra copies and then said she was going to make even more herself. "I can quietly slip a flyer into certain customers' bags," she said. "Of course, you and Elvis are always welcome in here. All well-behaved dogs are welcome. But I have to think that a dog might be a bit happier going on a quick walk with you than standing around here, especially when there are so many temptations here." I had to agree. Capers had some comfy-looking sofas and chairs for sale that might entice even the best-behaved dog to jump up and take a nap while his owner browsed.

"Did you hear about Ted's dog?" Two women carrying yoga mats walked through the door. My ears perked up. "Ted couldn't have been gone more than a couple of minutes and when he came out, Boris was gone," one woman said.

"I'm going to have to think twice before leaving Carly alone even for a second now," the other woman said.

"But it seems like it should be okay if you're just running in to get a cup of coffee or a gallon of milk," the other said.

Although I shared their sadness for Boris's disappearance, I have to admit I felt a little excited about my brilliant new approach to boosting my dog-walking business.

Mostly, though, I felt like I was lost, not Boris. I was completely lost about what to do next to find him.

CHAPTER 8

AFTER DINNER AND homework, Mom pulled some Metro bus schedules out of her tote bag and spread them on the counter for me.

"I'm way ahead of you on this one," I said. I'm a master of Seattle's Metro buses, with at least fourteen route schedules imbedded in my brain. This time I had actually been a little stumped on how to get across town going west to east. I used Metro's online trip planner and had checked "fewest transfers" as my preferred route. Fremont might be the Center of the Universe, but getting to Cesar Chavez Middle School from there wasn't going to be that easy. "I take the 26 or the 28 downtown to Third, then transfer to the 14. I get off the bus at seven thirty-four and have eleven minutes to get to school, which should be plenty of time because Chavez is only two blocks from the bus stop. At the end of the day I reverse my route, taking the 14 downtown and catching the 26 or the 28. Piece of cake." I threw that last part in for added reassurance.

Mom gave me a big hug and a smooch. I know she

constantly worries about me. I like to try to prove she can take it down a notch or two on the Worry Meter.

Monday morning went smoothly. Once again, my timing was perfect. The 14 pulled up just as I stepped off the 26. I made it to my locker and then to homeroom six minutes before the bell rang.

Mr. Park, my homeroom teacher, was trying to get one of those what-did-you-do-this-weekend conversations going. He looked at me.

"Um, not much. Just homework and stuff," I said, sliding down in my chair a bit, hoping he'd move on. He did.

Moving is a big deal, and almost anyone else in the world would have mumbled, "I moved." But Mom and I didn't want people—especially people at school—to know how often we moved. We couldn't risk some other parent challenging my right to go to Chavez since I didn't have a permanent address. A "right" permanent address, that is. Of course, we also didn't broadcast where we were house-sitting to protect the privacy of our clients.

Sometimes I use homeroom to race to finish last-minute details on homework. Sometimes I read. Today I was drawing Izzie and Elvis. Then I heard the word *Fremont*, and I snapped to attention.

"What did you do in Fremont?" Mr. Park asked Lily.

"Oh, you know. Just hung out. Hannah and I took her dog, I mean the dog of the people she's house-s . . . I mean dog-sitting." Lily was faltering, something that didn't happen that often. She sat up straighter as if collecting all her thoughts and going into Actress Mode. "We took a friend's dog for a walk around Fremont. I never really hung out there before. Do you go there, Mr. Park?"

Anyone who has been around Mr. Park for more than a day learns that all you have to do is ask him a question—instead of answering one of his questions—and you're safe from being called on for the rest of the day. He started talking about a summer solstice celebration, an outdoor film festival, the history of the Fremont area and the ship canal, the bus people statues, and the troll that lives under the bridge, and then the bell rang.

"We'll have to go back to Fremont sometime, okay, Hannah?" Lily said.

"Yeah. Right. Maybe this weekend," I said as we headed out to first period. Lily and I had endured an entire school year without having a single class, other than homeroom, together. We thought seventh grade would be our big chance because we each had four electives for the year. But Lily spent hers on jazz band and Spanish. I was using two electives to take Japanese all year, the third for advanced drawing, and the last one for animation.

Our school is huge, and the art room is on the exact opposite side of the school as Mr. Park's homeroom. I had to move fast to get there in time. Cesar Chavez Middle School is shaped like the letter *U*. Someone told me that if you went from one tip of the *U* to the other, it would be a quarter mile. I could go the interior route and get a quarter-mile walk in, or I could go out the back door of the school and cut across the garden, and then back inside to the hallway where the art rooms are. I always choose the outdoor route.

"I wasn't expecting this," said a voice next to me as we stepped out the back door. I know that Seattle has a reputation for raining all the time, but it doesn't really. Except now. It was a torrential downpour.

"Want to sprint?" I asked Jordan Walsh, the girl standing next to me. I knew Jordan was taking the same short cut— and not heading to one of the portable classrooms out back—because she's in my art class.

"Go!" she said, getting a split-second head start. But I made it to the other side of the garden first. I decided not to gloat about outpacing our school volleyball star. She might try to spike my head or something.

"Did you decide what to do for your theme?" Jordan asked as we got inside the art room. She was referring to our current art project. Our teacher, Mr. Van Vleck (he lets us call him V-2, as long as the principal isn't around) had given us an assignment he called "Studio Series 1." We were supposed to find a way to link a series of sketches together.

"I have no ideas," I said. "Do you?"

"No ideas. A big fat zero," she said, flopping her sketchbook onto the worktable.

There's nothing about Jordan that's a zero. She's tall, she's a great athlete, she's supersmart, and her family seems to have money to burn. I wouldn't say that Jordan and I are technically friends, but we keep getting thrown together in art classes and summer art camps. We also got thrown together last year when her mom was the toast of the town as an artist.

I opened my sketchbook and looked at what I'd done in the past few days. A picture of Izzie, a couple of Mango, one of Elvis, one of Boris, and another of Elvis. Dog doodles.

"Looks like you have a nice variety of subjects in your theme," Mr. Van Vleck said, glancing at my sketchbook.

I looked at him and at my drawings, then back at him, then back to my drawings. He'd already moved on by the time I squeaked out a "Thanks."

"And you said you didn't have any ideas," Jordan said.

"I didn't have any idea that I had ideas," I said truthfully. Once again, the answers were in my sketchpad. Apparently I'd selected dogs as my theme.

"You could do cats," I said. Jordan answered me with a "harrumph" noise.

I wish Advanced Drawing lasted all day. I like most of my classes, but I was happy to see the school day end. I walked out of the school and down the street to catch the Metro bus downtown. I got to the bus stop just as the 14 pulled up. I congratulated myself on my impeccable timing when it comes to Metro buses.

I climbed on board and settled into a seat near the window. Generally, I don't like it when people talk on their phones on buses, but it seemed acceptable to check my messages.

I had seven messages. "Whoa!" I must have said that out loud, because a woman across the aisle looked over at me. I gave her an apologetic shrug, and looked back at my phone. That many messages could mean that something was wrong, there was an emergency somewhere, there was someone who kept calling my number by mistake, or . . . my business was about to take off.

Fortunately, it was my business. It was booming. All seven callers inquired about my dog-walking services. Curiously, all seven callers also mentioned that Mack had sent them. Mack, that old crazy cat guy? Pretty nice of him.

CHAPTER 9

THREE THIRTY-ONE in the afternoon, and I was back in Fremont. I called Mom as soon as I got off the 26 bus, and then again when I got into the apartment. It's annoying to have to call her so many times, but it helps me keep my independence. This time she insisted that I wait until she got home before I called back any potential new clients. That was okay with me. I'd feel kind of stupid calling now and saying, "Um, I have to ask my mom. I'll call you back later." Not the kind of thing an entrepreneur would say.

I dumped my stuff on the kitchen table and grabbed Elvis's leash. He couldn't wait to get outside. I walked him down by the canal, and then we came back up to the shops. The yellow flyers and the green flyers were hard to miss. Every shop had them prominently displayed. Except The Perfect Pet. That was odd. Maybe they just hadn't put them up yet. Then I remembered that they hadn't had Boris's first missing flyer hanging up either. Maybe they had a policy against taping anything up.

The bell rang as Elvis and I opened the door to The

Perfect Pet. He barked—one deep, loud "woof" to announce our arrival.

Meredith, the volunteer I met at the animal shelter, came out to the counter. "Hi. I remember you said you were taking care of a basset hound," Meredith said. "Elvis is a regular here." Meredith seemed amped up today, especially compared to how she usually is at the animal shelter. I'd always thought of her as an extremely serious person. "You're Hannah, right? I'm good at dog names, usually, but I have a hard time remembering people's names. Now, Elvis has a card here, so we can give him a trim if you'd like."

I had no idea what she was talking about. "What do you mean by he has a 'card' here?"

"A nail card. You know," she looked at me expectantly. I must have returned a look that said, Huh?

"Elvis's owner, that tall, brown-haired woman? She pays in advance for nail trims for him. That way he can come in once every two weeks or so, and we cut his toenails. It's always important to keep a dog's nails short and trimmed, but it's especially important with a dog like this," she said. She lifted Elvis's front right paw. "See how large his paws are? There's a lot of weight that needs to be supported down here. The nails need to be cut or filed so that it's more comfortable for him. I'm surprised his owner didn't tell you all this. His file says that she's out of the country."

I sensed a tone of disapproval in Meredith's voice.

"I'm sure Piper, that's Elvis's owner, left all that information at home. I haven't gone through all of it yet," I said. Now Meredith's face wore a look of disapproval, perfectly in sync with her earlier tone. "I mean, I've gone through everything except the grooming information."

"Well, as long as you're here, we might as well trim those nails. It looks like it's been more than three weeks since he was last in. Really, he should be here every two weeks, three at the absolute outside." She looked at me expectantly.

"Okay. That would be great. What do I do?"

"You can stay here. We'll be right back."

I spent some time looking at tug toys, squeak toys, fetch toys, and chew toys. I think Piper had one of each model in a toy chest in her hall closet. She sure spent a lot of money on dog toys.

"Here's 'The King,'" Meredith said, using a nickname that I guessed was a reference to Elvis Presley, since I knew some people called him "the king of Rock and Roll."

"Great. Thanks. I need to buy some of those, too," I said, pointing to a box with a dozen rolls of Doggie Bags. "I'm starting a dog-walking business," I added, just in case she was wondering what I needed with 240 poop bags. "And some liver treats, too."

Meredith sighed. I thought maybe she was upset that I was choosing plastic bags for picking up dog poop. But really, what else was I supposed to use?

"I just don't get these people," she said, letting out another big sigh.

"What do you mean?"

"Dog walkers, dog sitters. No offense. I don't get why people have dogs if they can't walk them and spend time with them. Making a commitment to a dog should be a major life decision," she said.

"I'm sure it is a major life decision," I said. It was something that I picked up from an article that my mom had printed out from the Internet. Usually I don't pay any attention to her stuff—I just pass it along when she forgets to pick it up from the printer—but this time the name of the article caught my eye. It was called "Getting Along Gets Easier," and at first I thought it might be one of those parenting articles about how to get along with your troublesome teen. I know, technically I'm not a teen yet, but that's not the point. I was relieved to see that it was actually about getting along with difficult coworkers. One of the tips in the article was to repeat and agree with a neutral statement the person just made.

Just to drive the point home, I paraphrased what she said. "A dog is a huge commitment. We owe it to them to take proper care of them," I said in a most earnest voice.

Meredith nodded.

Elvis started sniffing around a recycling bin. "Elvis!" I said, giving him a tug on his leash. His snout emerged triumphantly with a candy bar wrapper stuck to it. I bent down to take it from him, and my eyes caught sight of bright green and yellow paper.

"You never can tell what people will put in recycling," I said. "I hope there's nothing else in there that isn't supposed to be." I rifled through the recycling basket, as if I were looking for another candy wrapper. Sure enough, I found them. Not candy wrappers, but the yellow flyer about Boris and the green flyer advertising my dog-walking business.

CHAPTER 10

"FIND ANYTHING ELSE down there?" Merideth asked. She leaned over the counter, her forehead and eyebrows scrunching up as she glared at me.

"Looks like the rest is all paper," I said, standing up. I couldn't figure out why someone would just toss those flyers aside. Unless . . . maybe it was good news.

"Do you know if anyone has found Boris?" I asked, but my voice was drowned out by Elvis's barking as the door to The Perfect Pet opened. A woman with a cinnamon-colored standard poodle—the biggest poodle—walked in.

"Well, hello to you, too, Elvis!" the woman said. Elvis immediately sat down and looked at her eagerly. He was in an I'm-a-good-dog-so-give-me-a-treat position. "Oh, you good boy. You want a treat, don't you?" She gave him a tasty reward.

"I'm sorry, I think I interrupted you," the woman said to me.

"Actually, I think Elvis interrupted me," I said. "I was just asking about Boris—"

"Such a sad thing, isn't it?" the woman said, this time really interrupting me. "We're all just worried sick about him. You probably saw the yellow flyer in our window." She turned to point to the window where, of course, there was no flyer. "Well, that's funny. I taped it up myself first thing this morning, and I'm sure it was there when I ran to PCC just now. Meredith, do you know where that flyer went?"

Meredith blushed. "No," she muttered.

"Boris is still missing," the woman said, turning her attention to me. "I just saw Ted at the grocery store. He's out of his mind with worry. Meredith, could you look up Ted's number? It's under 'B' for Boris. I'll need to call and tell him we need another flyer."

By now I'd caught on that this woman was the boss at The Perfect Pet.

"I helped Ted make the flyers, and I have some extras with me," I said, opening my messenger bag. I handed two to the woman. "Would you be willing to let me post my sign about my dog-walking business, too? I have references."

"Of course we can put that up! We had it up earlier, even though I didn't know who you were. I'm Arlene Helm, the owner of the shop here." She held out her hand to shake mine.

"I'm Hannah West. My mom and I are taking care of Piper Christenson's apartment for a few weeks," I said. "And Elvis. We're taking care of Elvis, too." I found a business card and handed it to her.

"Good to meet you. It's strange. I don't know what happened to those flyers," Arlene said, as she rummaged through a desk drawer to find some tape. "I know Meredith here isn't a big fan of people needing to hire someone to walk their dogs." She found the tape and picked up the flyers to put them in the window. While she was in the front of the store, Meredith grabbed both the garbage can and the recycling can. She mumbled something about taking them out back. Arlene was still talking. Then she shook her head. "Some people are much more comfortable with animals than with other people," she said. I assumed she was talking about Meredith.

I looked over to the window. That same guy with Scooter the shaggy dog was outside studying the yellow flyer. The bell on the door clattered as my canine charge and I hurried outside. I don't know why, but it felt like such a relief to be out of there.

"Hey! Wait up!" I called out to Shaggy-Dog Guy, who had started walking down the street.

"What were you doing outside The Perfect Pet just now?" I demanded once I caught up with him.

"Scooter was getting water. Is that a crime?" I could tell from his voice that he was just joking.

Scooter sniffed me, and I scratched him behind his ears. "No, of course not. I just wondered why you were so interested in those signs. I thought maybe you had a lead on locating Boris."

"I was kind of hoping that Boris had been found already," he said. "See this poster for Boris? I noticed that it's different than the one that was up before. But I guess I'll keep looking."

"Are you hoping to get the reward money for Boris?" I asked.

"I wouldn't turn it down," he said. "But mostly I just want to help Boris. Do you know him?"

"Actually, no. Not yet, anyway. My mom and I met his owner. I helped him redo the poster. That one's mine, too," I said, pointing to the green one.

"That's cool."

"I'm Hannah, by the way. And I guess you already know Elvis."

"I'm Benito. But most people call me Ben," he said.

"You live around here?" I asked. I know that sounds totally corny, but I was in my detective mode of gathering information. "I thought you had to be in your twenties or thirties to live in Fremont."

"You live here. And you're not that old," he said. Crafty. He not only wasn't answering my question, he was turning it around. I decided to play along.

"I don't really live here. I just work here. You know, walking dogs and taking care of other things," I said.

"Do you go to Jefferson Middle School?"

"No. I go to Chavez." If I'd really lived in Fremont, I probably would be going to Jefferson. Elvis whined. He was done sniffing Scooter, and he wanted to get moving. "Apparently Elvis here wants to go up that hill."

"Scooter and I are going up to Market Time. I need a Snickers," he said.

Snickers! Any doubts I had about this guy immediately vanished with that one magic word.

"Are you kidding? Is there a place around here to buy real candy? I thought it would all be made of tofu and wheat germ or something," I said. The prospect of all that chewy nougat and caramel goodness covered in milk chocolate had me pretty excited.

"Haven't you been to Market Time yet?" he asked. I shook my head no. "I'll show you where it is. It's a big walk up the hill, but it's worth it. The owners are cool."

On the way up the street, Ben told me about the owners of Market Time. "They used to be hippies," he said, "but they're both total chocoholics. They can totally appreciate the need for a real candy bar."

When we reached the store, Ben and I took turns going inside so that one person was always outside with the dogs. Ben said he leaves Scooter outside all the time, and he thought it was perfectly safe. Still, I didn't want to take any chances. Especially since I was trying to get my new business off the ground.

It seemed like everyone in Fremont knew Ben, Scooter, or Elvis—or all three. But I got a few strange looks. I guess people were wondering what a stranger was doing with Piper's dog. Fremont is the kind of neighborhood where people look out for one another. Clearly that included looking out for dogs, especially since one had disappeared recently. People were curious about me, and even more curious once they found out that I was a legitimate dog walker taking care of Elvis. It actually turned out to be good for business. Having been hired by Piper was a great recommendation. But getting Ben's endorsement seemed like the best advertising of all.

"Are you the one who has the signs posted about dog-walking and pet-sitting?" a woman with a small wheat-colored dog asked.

I handed her my business card.

"Elvis is in good hands with Hannah," Ben said.

"I'll give you a call. I'd like to talk with your parents, too," the woman said.

And you can bet my mom is going to want to talk with you, too, I thought. And with everyone else who calls.

"I'll usually have Elvis with me, so I can walk your dog after school if your dog gets along with Elvis," I said again and again, handing out my business cards.

"How come you know so many people?" I asked.

"Everyone knows my grandfather around here, so they kind of end up knowing me, too."

We kept heading downhill, handing out business cards

to anyone who showed any interest in my business. Some people who didn't even have dogs took one, telling me they were going to pass it along to a friend.

When we got back near the canal, I noticed Mack, across the street, talking animatedly with Ted, Boris's owner. They shook hands and then Mack tipped his hat. It seemed to be his trademark. Ted walked away, and Mack spotted us and waved from across the street. I waved back.

"Do you know Mack?" I asked Ben. "I see him everywhere."

Ben laughed just as my cell phone rang. No doubt it was my mom calling to remind me to get home and do homework. "Well," I told Ben, "Elvis got a longer walk than he expected. Now my mom—and my homework—are calling."

"See you later," he said. As I answered my phone, he crossed the street to talk to Mack in front of Costas Opa, the Greek restaurant on the corner of Thirty-fourth and Fremont.

CHAPTER 11

DID I SAY business was booming? I *should* have said business could potentially be booming. Although I had a bunch of calls about my availability as a dog walker, the Maggie West Inquiry System was holding me up. My mom wanted to talk to everyone first, and then she wanted to make arrangements for both of us to meet the canines and their owners. To further complicate it, I had ultimate Frisbee practice two days a week after school. Our school gets out superearly, so even with a two-hour practice and two buses, I could be home shortly after five o'clock.

We spent several days talking with dog owners and setting up times to meet that next weekend.

I was working on a new sketch of Elvis on Thursday night. He's a great model—a master at staying still. I had almost as many sketches of him as I had of Izzie. But I never got tired of sketching either of them. I get kind of lost when I'm drawing. My sixth-grade art teacher told us it was "flow." She said it was this state of concentration when you have all this positive energy because you're enjoying yourself and you're totally absorbed in what you're doing. I'm not sure if I was totally lost in my drawing or in flow or what, but I seriously jumped when my cell phone rang and interrupted me. I didn't recognize the number, but the businesswoman in me decided to answer anyway.

"Hello, is this the number for the dog walker? I saw a flyer at Fremont Place Books," a woman said.

"Yes! That's me. I mean, I'm the dog walker. My name is Hannah West, and I'm extremely responsible. I've walked all kinds and all sizes of dogs, and I know a lot about dogs. I have references you can contact, if you'd like. Is there something I can help you with?" I was talking about a million miles a minute.

"Well, I normally walk Archie three times a day, but lately I've been getting home from work late, and I really think Archie would like some human interaction earlier than that. I'm actually looking for someone who could take him out in the mid- to late afternoon," she said.

"That's me! I mean, I can easily do that. I get out of school at two-fifteen, and I think I'll be home by three thirty or so. Would that work?"

"Oh, you're a student? Where do you go to school?" she asked. I figured this was a polite way of getting the information she really wanted to know: my age.

"I'm in seventh grade at Cesar Chavez Middle School. I walk dogs as an after-school and weekend job," I explained.

"I guess that might work. Could I check all this out with

one of your parents?" she asked. I passed my phone to Mom, who talked *waaaay* too long with my new client. At last she handed the phone back to me.

"I didn't know you were staying in Piper's apartment," the woman, whose name was Nikki, said. "Elvis and Archie are great friends. I worked some things out with Maggie, and, if you're up for it, you could bring Elvis over here and pick up Archie and take them both for a walk after school. Everyone around here knows Elvis and Archie, so people will be looking out for you."

I completely forgot to ask what kind of dog Archie was. I'd be meeting him soon enough, because Nikki, my newest client, lived in the apartment building across the alley from us. Mom was taking me (and I was taking Elvis) over right away to meet Nikki and Archie, and to get a key and instructions.

I am happy to report that Archie is the sweetest bulldog that has ever walked on this planet. He and Elvis were excited to see each other. At least I think they were excited. If you know anything about bulldogs and bassets, you know that they don't show a lot of emotion in their wrinkly faces.

When we got back to our apartment, Mom pulled out some paper and started mapping out a calendar. I'd agreed to walk Archie every day. Even the late walks on Tuesday and Thursday turned out to be okay with Nikki, who said they would allow her to stay downtown and take a yoga class before heading home. I'd walk him right after school on Mondays, Wednesdays, and Fridays, starting the next day, Friday. Then I'd meet all the other dogs and set up their schedules over the weekend.

I put Archie's apartment key on my key ring and into my messenger bag. Then I got everything ready for school the next day. I'm not the most organized person in the world, but I like to have things in order before I go to sleep. I crawled into bed with my sketchpad, quickly drawing Archie. I wasn't exactly in that flow zone my art teacher had talked about, but I was feeling pretty good. It turns out Archie was the missing link in my Studio Series for my drawing class. I had five dogs in a whole series of expressions and stances that I felt pretty happy about. I hoped Mr. Van Vleck would be happy about it. It's nice to be an artist, but it's even better to be an artist with good grades.

CHAPTER 12

"DO YOU ACTUALLY know all those dogs?" Jordan asked. We were showing each other our plans for the Studio Series. "Or did you just check out a dog book and start drawing?"

"Yeah, I know them. I've taken care of almost all of them," I said, pointing out Izzie, Ruff, Mango, Elvis, and Archie. Okay, I hadn't actually taken care of Archie yet, but he was one of my clients. And helping Ted with the flyers for Boris was kind of like taking care of him.

"Do you actually know all those staplers?" I asked. For some reason, Jordan had chosen office supplies as her theme. You heard me: ordinary office supplies. Paper clips, a tape dispenser, a pencil cup, and more than a few staplers. I had to admit it was a rather brilliant idea. If I didn't like the way my dog series was shaping up, I'd wish I'd thought of something as commonplace as office supplies.

"All of my ideas led to dead ends. Then last night I was looking for a pencil sharpener in my dad's den. It took me a while to find it, but it was like he could open a stapler museum. Every drawer I opened had a stapler in it. It seemed kind of funny to me at the time. It's not as funny today," she said.

"I think it works," I said. "It's . . . different."

She snorted.

"Different is good," I added.

"Riiiiight," Jordan said, stretching out the one syllable so it lasted about five extra beats. Lily and I had thoroughly analyzed Jordan over the past few months. She wasn't exactly the kind of girl who would think different was good, unless she was differentiated from the popular girls as being the *most* popular girl.

Mr. Van Vleck called us up one by one for quick conferences about our projects. He gave me eight out of eight points and told me to keep going. He spent longer with Jordan. She came back to the table looking relaxed and happy.

"What are you doing this weekend?" she asked, as we gathered our supplies at the end of the period. "You've got a game, right?"

"We have a game tomorrow morning. Then I'm spending some time with my dogs," I said. "How about you? Where's your game?"

"It's over at McKinley," she said. "Then I'm going to spend some time getting to know my staplers."

Was it possible that Jordan and I were becoming friends? I wondered.

Nah. We were just talking, finding common ground in our shared interest in art and sports—volleyball for her and ultimate Frisbee for me.

I kept thinking ahead the rest of the school day, anxious to get home to take Archie out for a walk.

And finally, at 3:33, I was back in Fremont. I dutifully called my mom when I got off the bus, when I got into the apartment (she insisted that I stay on the line while I got Elvis and his leash and left the apartment), when I got to Archie's apartment, and when I—finally—headed out with my two canine clients. All this calling is excessive, if you ask me.

For a short guy, Elvis was pretty strong. He practically pulled me across the alley and up the stairs to Archie's apartment. It was as if the two dogs hadn't seen (or sniffed) each other in ages.

It must have been pretty entertaining to see a bulldog and a basset walking down the street, because we got lots of attention. More attention than I like to get. I reminded myself it was the dogs, not me, that people were ogling.

I walked past the scene of the crime—Joe's Special. The bright yellow flyer for Boris and the green flyer for my business were still in the window. I wondered if that meant Boris hadn't come home in the time I'd been at school.

A noise startled me. Meredith was inside The Perfect Pet, rapping on the glass. She beckoned me in.

"This bulldog certainly looks familiar," she said in a singsong voice. "How are you, Arnold?"

"You're great, aren't you, Archie?" I said, cleverly correcting her about his name without embarrassing her. Or so I hoped.

"Oh! I called you the wrong name, didn't I, little guy?" she gushed. Meredith was kind of hyper again. And she seemed a little too interested in Archie. It made me a little uncomfortable.

"Any news about Boris?" I asked, hoping to take the focus off Archie. When she didn't respond, I added, "The missing bichon frise?"

"Hmm? No. No news today. Did you know we do cat grooming here, too? We have special hours just for cats so they won't be stressed by being around dogs."

She kept prattling on. I had no idea why she was talking about cats or why she was talking so much in the first place. I find that sometimes it's best not to try making sense of what adults do when they act strange. I remembered what Arlene said about Meredith being better with animals than people. Maybe this is what she was referring to.

"Sorry. What?" I realized Meredith had finally stopped talking and was looking at me, as if waiting for an answer. Her eyes shifted, and I followed her gaze outside.

"I hope that missing dog is found soon," she mumbled in a sudden mood change. I had no idea what made her personality change so quickly. I looked outside again. Mack was in front of The Perfect Pet. He tipped his hat as if to say hello, and then wandered off.

CHAPTER 13

"IT'S PAYDAY!" Mom said, swinging the door open and interrupting my thoughts. Elvis immediately jumped down from the couch and went to the door for a belly rub. "Let's go to Blue C Sushi."

She didn't need to say anything else. Blue C was my absolute favorite restaurant, and living in Fremont meant it was just steps away. I pulled a hooded sweatshirt over my head and grabbed my sketchbook.

"Back soon," I said to Elvis.

Blue C Sushi means instant gratification. There's no wait to order or to get food. You sit at a counter and a conveyor belt a few inches above the counter carries little plates of sushi around the restaurant. If you see something you like, you grab it and put it on your tabletop. There's room for about forty people around the conveyor belt. I hoped we were early enough so we could get two spots together right away.

"Two of you?" the man at the door asked. Mom nodded, and he started to lead us to the counter. He stopped and said to her, "Does she need the green chopsticks?"

"No, she doesn't," I said, replying for my mom. Geesh. I hate it when adults don't speak directly to kids. They talk to your parent as if you're not even there. And I must say I was greatly offended that he thought I, of all people, would need the chopsticks that they give little kids (they're supposed to be easier to handle). I've been a chopstick master since I was four years old, and it's not just because I'm Chinese.

"Hey, listen, I'm sorry I did that," the guy said, this time speaking directly to me. "I hate it when people don't speak directly to kids."

This guy wasn't so bad after all, especially since he just said what was in my head.

"Now, remember we like green and yellow best. Especially green," Mom said, once we were seated.

I knew exactly what she meant. At conveyor belt sushi places, they figure out how much you owe for your food by counting your plates at the end of the meal. The plates are color coded for price. At Blue C Sushi, the yellow and green plates are the cheapest. If you avoided the dark blue plates, you could eat supercheap here. It was easy for me, because most of my favorites were also the least expensive. I went for the *kappa-maki* (rice and cucumber rolled inside seaweed; green plate) and spicy noodles (yellow plate). With tea, my dinner was less than five dollars.

"Doesn't that boy over there look familiar?" Mom asked.

I looked up from my sketch pad. He sure did. I knew the

guy in the next seat, too. It was Ben and Mack. Were they together? I didn't think so. Ben looked like he was doing homework, and Mack was talking to one of the sushi chefs. I looked at the person on the other side of Ben. It was a man about my mom's age, who I assumed was Ben's dad.

My mom's friend, Lisa, came over to us. "Maggie!" she cried. "I heard you were house-sitting for Piper. And I heard you, Miss Hannah, are the talk of the neighborhood."

"What?" Mom asked, sounding a bit alarmed.

"I saw the signs advertising a dog-walking business, and one of my neighbors just handed me your card. She said she met you with Benito, up at Market Time." After that I tuned them out as they gossiped about former coworkers. I went back to sketching.

"I'll have Hannah call you to set up a time when she can meet your dog," Mom said, nudging me with her toes.

"Right," I said, snapping to attention. "I'm very attentive and responsible."

Lisa and Mom said good-bye, and then Mom turned back to me. "Benito—is that the boy we met with the shaggy dog?" she asked. "I wish we knew a little more about him."

"Maybe we can go talk to him now," I said, but when we looked across to the other side of the counter, Ben was gone. So was the guy I assumed was his dad. Mack was just getting up, fishing some money out of his wallet to leave on the counter. He put his hat on and headed out, holding the restaurant door open to allow a group of older girls to come in.

"Oh, you guys! I found the most adorable teacup puppy on the Internet! He only weighs two pounds, and I think I'm going to get him!" one of the girls said.

"You *must* tell us the site where you found your dog," another girl said.

"I can't decide if I want a brown or a black dog," a third girl said.

"Black goes with everything," one replied.

"Brown is the new black." They all laughed. My *kappa-maki* suddenly felt heavy in my stomach. I couldn't believe that real people thought of their dogs as accessories. I thought that was just something you read about in magazines or see on TV.

We headed back to the apartment to get Elvis then took him for a walk together. We walked up the hill a couple of blocks. "Whoa! Where did that come from?" I asked, staring at a huge mansion up the street. It was such a surprise to see that big of a house in a neighborhood where it was mostly apartment buildings and businesses. The yard must have taken up at least half a city block. An iron fence ran around the perimeter of the property.

"I forgot about this place. I don't remember who owns it, but supposedly an eccentric old man and an army of cats live there."

A dog barked, and we heard a screen door close somewhere in the back of the house.

"I wonder how the army of cats likes that dog," I said.

CHAPTER 14

"I HAVE A surprise for you in the car," Mom said after my Frisbee game Saturday morning. I felt a total sense of déjà vu, like I was living last Saturday all over again.

My team, the Chavez Bulldogs, had just beaten Jefferson Middle School, the school close to Fremont where Ben goes. I didn't really expect Ben to be on their team, but I was kind of hoping he was.

"Is the surprise a drooling dog with droopy ears?" I asked.

"That's just a bonus," she said, unlocking the car trunk. She pulled a maple bar and a frosty blue Gatorade out of a grocery bag and handed them to me. "Great job, honey. I'm proud of you." She gave me a hug.

"And you're the best mom ever," I said, immediately taking a bite of the maple bar. I felt it was my responsibility to consume the pastry as quickly as possible before I got in the car and had to protect it from Elvis.

There wasn't enough time for me to change my clothes before my volunteer shift at the animal shelter. I pulled a hooded sweatshirt over my head and changed from my cleats to regular sneakers.

"Hi, Meredith," I said as we practically collided in the doorway at the Elliott Bay Animal Shelter. She kept going, walking hurriedly to a blue car in the parking lot. I think the tires even screeched as she drove off, but that could have been in my head. She seemed to be in such a hurry that I imagined the tires screeching and gravel spurting out from under the tires.

"Hannah, can I see you?" Leonard asked as I was signing in. I followed him back to a small office. "I need to let you know that Izzie's gone."

I don't know what my face looked like, but it must have been pretty traumatized.

"No, no, no! I didn't mean it that way," Leonard rushed to say. "Gosh, I'm sorry. I just meant that Izzie has a new home."

"But that's a great thing! That's the best thing that could happen!"

"Of course it is. I just thought you'd be sad not to be able to see her today," he said.

I was sad, and I knew Leonard could tell that I was fighting back tears. Geesh! I wanted to kick myself for being so selfish. Our whole goal was to find good homes for animals.

"Did she—" I started.

"Yes," he said reassuringly. "She definitely went to a

good home. A nice family adopted her. It was a good match all the way around."

"Thanks for telling me," I said. Leonard got up and started to head down the hall. "Wait!" I called after him. I opened my sketchbook and looked at the drawings of Izzie. I quickly reviewed them, and almost had to kick myself again for being selfish. I wanted to keep the best one for myself, but I forced myself to tear it from the book. "Here," I said, handing it to Leonard. "Do you think it would be possible to give Izzie's new family this picture of her?"

Leonard studied the drawing. "I'm sure they'll be honored and thrilled to have this," he said.

I met some great dogs during the next three hours, but I realized I was holding something back, as if I was afraid of getting too attached to one of them.

When my shift was over, I practically collided with Meredith in the doorway—again. Another déjà vu.

"We meet again," I said. I thought I was rather funny, but Meredith just barreled past me. Whatever.

At least Elvis was happy to see me. Once we got back to the apartment building after our walk, we took the elevator to the fourth floor. The doors were just starting to open when Elvis bolted, galloping down the hallway.

"Elvis!" I cried, running after him. I stopped when I saw what had him so excited. He was licking a little white curly-haired dog. A bichon frise.

"Boris?" I asked.

"Yes! It's Boris! I just got him back," Ted said.

"That's great! I'm so happy for you. When did you get him back?" I asked.

"Only about an hour ago." Ted picked Boris up. "I was just taking him for a little walk. I'm never letting him out of my sight again. Unless, of course, it's with a responsible dog walker like you."

"Will he let me pick him up?" I asked.

"Of course. He's as gentle and compliant as they get."

I picked up the white ball of fluff named Boris and cuddled him. He was absolutely adorable. He even smelled cute.

"He smells like you just gave him a lavender bath," I said, rubbing my nose in his neck.

"He is rather spotless, now that you mention it. He doesn't seem to be affected by what happened, either. He's calm and happy."

"Where was he? How did you get him back?" I asked.

Suddenly Ted, who'd been chatty and relaxed just a moment ago, was in an ultra rush. He scooped Boris out of my arms. "Oh, that doesn't matter," he said hurriedly. "The important thing is that he's back. Gotta go!" he called, heading toward the elevator.

Was I imagining it, or was he avoiding my question?

CHAPTER 15

MOM HELPED ME work out dog details over the weekend. She finished prescreening all my clients—the human clients—and took me to meet each dog and its owner. Archie and Elvis were the only ones getting a walk every weekday. But I had plenty of other dogs on all the other days; some were just once a week, some twice, and others three times a week.

"I hope you can still fit me into your busy afterschool schedule," Lily said on Wednesday morning, looking down at the calendar Mom had helped me set up. "Let's see, I can squeeze you in right after school, but I've got Archie, Sadie, and Otis this afternoon, too. Not to mention Elvis."

"Wow. How many canine clients do you have now?" Lily said, trying to make sense of the rather complicated schedule I had. Each day had the names of the dogs who needed walks, and each dog had an entry with the owner's name, address, phone number, and what kind of exercise the dog needed. "Is Elvis going to be able to keep up with you?"

"It's a myth that bassets are lazy and fat. They actually have incredible endurance. Elvis could walk twenty miles a day if he had his way. He has no problem keeping up. In fact, you might have a problem keeping up with him."

She rolled her eyes at me. "I'll meet you at your locker," she said, fishing a Metro bus ticket out of her pocket and then stuffing it back in again.

After school and two bus rides, Lily and I dropped our things in Piper's apartment and took Elvis down the hall to pick up Sadie, a cocker spaniel. Next stop was Archie's.

"We need to pick up one more after this. You can take two dogs and I'll take two dogs," I said.

We went and got Otis, a gray miniature schnauzer from the same building where Archie lived. We took the dogs to the path by the canal first, so they could sniff and do their business. Then Lily wanted to walk around the shops, so we headed back.

The dogs took a communal drink at the dog bowl in front of Joe's and The Perfect Pet.

"Is that store ever open?" asked Lily, nodding toward the "Closed" sign in the window of The Perfect Pet.

"Of course it's open. Sometimes, that is," I read the sign with its hours. "It just doesn't appear to be open when it says it will be."

"Let's take all the dogs home and then see what kind of snack food your mom bought," Lily said.

I was about to tell her that my mom's idea of junk food

these days wasn't exactly in line with the needs of two hungry girls, but I didn't get a chance to say anything.

"She's gone!" a woman screamed. "She . . . just . . . disappeared."

CHAPTER 16

ABOUT A HALF-dozen people gathered around the woman outside a store called London's. I had to stand back a bit because I had a dog—or two—with me. Unfortunately, the woman who screamed didn't have a dog with her. That was the problem.

"I just went back to my car to get my glasses out of the glove compartment. I left Daphne right here because she seemed so content," the woman said, practically hyperventilating. "When I came back, she was gone. I called for her a few times, but someone must have taken her. Her leash is gone, too."

Elvis barked, which startled everyone. He pulled at the leash, wanting to go down Thirty-fourth Street. He somehow signaled Archie and the other two to start pulling as well. I held my ground.

"Excuse me," I said through the crowd. "What kind of dog is Daphne? We can help you look for her."

"She's a pom-poo—you know, a Pomeranian-poodle mix."

I could sort of imagine what a dog like that might look

like, but not exactly. "Do you have a picture?" I asked.

"Of course," the woman said. She pulled a photo out of her wallet. Mack, the old guy in the bowler hat, took it from her. He looked intently at the photo, nodding. He passed the photo to the next person, and it finally made its way to Lily and me. A little brown speck of a dog was pictured with a shopping-mall Santa. "Daphne is about eight pounds. She's tan with dark brown markings. She has a brown spot around one eye and a brown tip on one ear. She's absolutely adorable. Oh, what am I going to do? I need to stay here in case she comes back, but I need to look for her, too."

"Oh, Jennifer, this is so horrible. Just like when Boris disappeared," a man said.

"Boris made it back safely, though," Lily said.

"We can help you look right now," I offered.

The woman looked at me skeptically. I told her I'd made the flyer for Ted and that I'd be happy to do the same for her. She gave me another skeptical look.

"I know Ted offered a big reward," she said. "Even though she means the world to me, I'm not sure I can do that."

"I don't think reward money will be necessary," Mack said.

"But it couldn't hurt," Lily added.

The woman wrote down her name and phone number for me, and I handed her my card.

Chapter 17

Two missing dogs in less than two weeks. A coincidence? I don't think so. There were too many things in common. Both were little dogs. Portable dogs. Each weighed less than ten pounds. Someone could pick either one up and tuck it under a coat or into a bag and just walk away. Someone could even run away because the dogs were so small.

Each time the owner had been just steps away from the scene of the crime. Conceivably, the dog owners could have come back at any time, interrupting the crime. Unless the dognapper knew the owners' habits so well that the dognapper could anticipate how long the owner would be gone.

I wanted to know more about pom-poos. After Lily and I ate all the soy nuts and pears in the house, she headed home and I headed for my laptop.

Pom-poos are sometimes called pomapoos or pooranians. This mixed breed was half toy poodle and half Pomeranian. Crossing dogs with poodles seemed to be getting more and more popular. Last summer I'd taken care of a wonderful Labrador/poodle mix—a labradoodle—named Mango. In the small dog world, people were going poo crazy. There were yorkie-poos (Yorkie and poodle), shih-poos (shih tzu and poodle), schnoodles (miniature schnauzer and poodle), cock-apoo (cocker spaniel and poodle), and many other dogs with a "poo" tacked onto their mix. I was momentarily distracted by a Web site that advertised "Designer Dogs," where people were offering chugs (chihuhua and pug mix) and pugles (pug and beagle mix).

Designer dogs? I flashed back to the college-aged girls I'd overheard at the sushi restaurant. They'd been talking about choosing a dog based on what color would look best with their outfits. "Brown is the new black," one had said. They'd also said they were shopping for dogs on the Internet, as if the dogs were shoes you'd order from an online store.

Designer dogs also made me think of celebrities carrying small dogs around as if the dog were a fashion accessory. It turns out that there are dog fashions just like there are clothing fashions. When I was little, dalmatians were all the rage because of a movie (I think you can guess which one) featuring the white dogs with black spots. A few years later, pugs were superpopular based on a movie with a pug named Frank. Chihuahuas and teacup dogs all became popular because of movies, TV, or celebrities.

Now there was a booming business of shifty people

selling little dogs on the Internet. You could buy a dog without ever meeting it. The dog would then be put on a plane and sent to you. I could see that there was some serious money in dealing little puppies. But would people pay as much for a full-grown dog? Pugnapping seemed to be a popular endeavor for crooked canine thieves. If you have a pug, you can't even leave him or her in your front yard to romp freely because someone could reach over the fence, pass the pug to a partner in a pickup, then speed away.

Boris and Daphne were even more portable than pugs. They had a high price on their heads if sold. And, of course, there was the substantial reward money Ted had offered for Boris's safe return.

It was getting late, especially for a school night. Mom was still downtown working at Wired Café. A beep told me I had a new e-mail. It was from Ben. I had given him my e-mail address so he could let me know about any potential clients he might have for me.

**Did you hear that another dog is missing?
My grandpa says it's a little white
Pomeranian named Daphne. You should
make another flyer. If you want, that is.
Scooter says "hi."
See you later.
Ben.**

CHAPTER 18

"EVERYBODY THINKS I have something to do with it!" I whined to mom when she finally got home.

"I doubt that's true. Why don't you let me listen to the messages?"

I handed my cell phone over to her. She took notes as she listened to each message.

"Well—" she started to say.

"They think, since we're new in the neighborhood, that I'm using my dog-walking business as a cover to get close to the dogs," I said.

"I'm not sure that's true . . ." Mom said.

"Then why did all my Thursday and Friday clients cancel?"

"They didn't all cancel. You still have Archie. And Elvis, of course."

"But the others? They don't think they can trust me," I said. I wasn't sure if I was mad or sad. Both, I decided. I was definitely mad that people would jump to conclusions, and

I was sad that those conclusions implicated me as having something to do with the two missing dogs.

Okay, so no one came right out and said: "We've seen you around the neighborhood with dogs that aren't yours. You seemed to appear right about the time that the dognappings started. You obviously have something to do with it, and we absolutely cannot trust you with our pets."

"Hannah, listen to me," Mom interrupted the tirade in my head. "People are just saying they're worried about their dogs. They sounded genuinely concerned for you, as well. If someone is really dognapping these dogs, they certainly don't want a young girl to be in the middle of it. After listening to those messages, I don't want you in the middle of it, either. You could get hurt."

This time it was my turn to listen to the messages again. People were worried about their dogs and didn't want them out of their sight. But I still think two or three people had a tone of voice that was a bit accusatory. New girl arrives; dogs disappear. Never mind that Boris disappeared hours before we moved in. Or that he'd been returned.

Speaking of which, I asked Mom if she'd heard anything from Ted about where Boris had been or who collected the reward money.

"I've run into him a few times, but he's always on his cell phone," she said. "Come to think of it, a couple times he pulled the phone out when he saw me. Of course, it could have just rung."

I'd used that trick to avoid talking to people several times myself.

For some reason, Ted didn't want to tell us the details about Boris's disappearance and return. Granted, we weren't old friends or anything, but why would he pointedly avoid talking about it?

I told myself that it was good that business had slowed down, although "screeched to a halt" would be a more accurate way to phrase it. I had an ultimate Frisbee tournament on Saturday that involved teams from half of Washington State. In fact, I was going to have to skip volunteering at the animal shelter this weekend. And, of course, there's always that little thing called homework.

Still, it was pretty depressing to think that my business had blossomed and died in the space of about forty-eight hours. I was down to just two dogs to walk after school on Friday. I called Nikki to make sure she wanted me to walk Archie.

"Absolutely. He loves your after-school walks," she said. "Unless you don't want to walk him anymore." She sounded worried, as if I might not like her dog.

"I love walking Archie. It's just that, well, honestly, a few of my clients have canceled. I think they're worried about the dognappings," I said. "I mean, they have every right to be worried. But I don't see how canceling an exercise date for your dog with someone as responsible as I am can help keep your dog safe. I just want to be sure that you feel okay leaving Archie with me."

Nikki laughed. "You don't have to sell me on how responsible you are. To tell you the truth, all dog owners in the area are a little freaked out. I feel like more than ever I need someone who will keep an eye on my Archie. Don't let people freaking out freak you out."

Nikki told me she'd set up an account with The Perfect Pet. "If you feel like taking Archie in for a nail trim one of these days, that would be great."

I put the finishing touches on a flyer for Daphne and e-mailed it to Jennifer. She was going to copy it and put it up right away, before people headed out to work the next morning. By the time I headed to the bus stop to catch the 28, there were orange flyers advertising Daphne's disappearance in the places that Boris's flyer once occupied. As my bus pulled away, I caught a glimpse of Jennifer coming out of Peet's Coffee with Mack. They shook hands, and he did his customary tip-of-the-hat gesture.

My cell phone vibrated almost immediately. I don't like to talk on the phone when I'm on a bus, but I recognized Jennifer's number.

"Hello?" I whispered, trying to be discreet.

"It's Jennifer. Are you still at home? I need to make a change to the flyer," she said. "It's imperative that we make it clear that there is a significant reward for Daphne's return."

I resisted the urge to ask how much "significant" equaled in terms of dollars, but not only was that none of my business, it wasn't actually important. It's just interesting that she'd so sorrowfully said the day before that she couldn't offer a cash reward. In fact, she'd said that maybe she could scrounge up "fifty dollars or so after the weekend." Why the sudden change? Had she sold a family heirloom or something?

I told her I was already on a bus heading downtown.

"That's okay. I have a pen with me. Maybe I'll get more attention if I add the note about the reward in handwriting."

"I could do it after school," I offered.

"No, thanks. I need to do it now. Ted made it pretty clear to me that the only way he got Boris back was because of the cash reward he offered. I've got to get started," she said. "Thanks."

She hung up.

Had Boris really been dognapped? Had the dognappers threatened to snatch him again? Maybe that's why Ted was being so secretive about Boris's return.

I was glad he could give Jennifer some advice that might get her dog home sooner.

CHAPTER 19

IT RAINED ALL weekend, which made the all-day Frisbee tournament on Saturday a little less fun. But only a little less, because it was still superfun to get to play five games in one day. Winning four of those games added a little bit to the fun factor.

Mom had the weekend off to watch my games and spend what she called "downtime" with me. Thanks to the steady supply of Seattle rain, we spent most of that downtime inside.

By Sunday night, there was still no news about Daphne, even though Jennifer had made it abundantly clear that a reward was being offered. "Substantial REWARD!!" was written in bold, black marker on each of the orange signs.

Maybe money wasn't the answer.

After dinner on Sunday, Mom and I took the dog out for a short walk, zigzagging our way back and forth through the main Fremont streets. We stopped at the steps of the Lenin statue for Elvis to do some extra sniffing. Having a statue of a former Communist leader on display as public art was controversial at first, but the general consensus now was that it was a beautifully crafted statue that ignited some healthy political conversations. At least that's what I read in the History of Fremont Web page.

A familiar-looking woman sat on a nearby bench, holding a red umbrella. I think she jinxed the weather because all of a sudden it started dumping rain.

"Let's get home!" Mom said. But Elvis took that exact moment to stop and, as they say, "do his business." I waited patiently (or not so patiently) for him to finish, but Elvis was taking his time.

As we watched, a man in a yellow rain slicker and matching rain hat approached her. The woman with the red umbrella stood up, and I thought again there was something familiar about her. The man reached out and they shook hands quickly. Then the woman stuffed her hands into her pockets, and the man quickly tucked his hands under his arms. Weird. Were they just trying to stay dry, or was there something else going on? The woman turned quickly, then scurried away in the rain. The man in the slicker looked toward us. I couldn't see his face because his hat was pulled low. But I did see him reach up and move the brim up and down in one smooth motion, as if tipping his hat.

"Was that Mack?" I said, voicing my thoughts out loud.

At the same time, Mom said, "If I didn't know better, I'd say that looked like a ransom drop."

The word *ransom* made me think of Jennifer and her urgency about the reward. Suddenly I realized why the woman with the umbrella had seemed familiar. I was pretty sure it *was* Jennifer.

There was a loud clap of thunder, and it started raining even harder. Part of me wanted to stay to figure out what was really going on, but the more rational part of me was busy concentrating on getting out of the rain as quickly as possible.

Back in Piper's apartment, we sat at the kitchen counter drying off and sipping warm cups of peppermint tea. Mom refused to listen to my theories about the dognapping case. She was too busy enjoying the fact that someone named Mack was wearing what she called a "mack." She said that was the word Brits used for a rubberized rain jacket. She started singing a song I recognized from the Beatles.

Parents are so easily amused. And so weird.

I went to bed, but I couldn't stop thinking about Mack and Jennifer.

That Wednesday, Lily came home with me after school. It was raining again, but this time it was a light rain, the kind of rain we get most often in Seattle. It's not enough to deal with the hassle of an umbrella, but it's a constant drizzle that's less than pleasant. Elvis and Archie were with us, and, true Seattle dogs that they are, they didn't seem to mind the rain.

"Let's walk under the bridge for a ways to stay drier," Lily suggested.

"Whoa! I didn't know he was going to be right here! I remember him totally freaking me out as a kid," I said, as we walked toward the famous Fremont Troll. I hadn't been to see it since we'd lived there, and it wasn't because I was still scared. I had promised Mom that I wouldn't go under the bridge alone, just in case an unsavory sort was hiding under there, but I don't think she meant this piece of public art.

"He's not as scary close up as he used to be," Lily said. "He's actually almost cute. I was petrified of him when I was little."

I thought he still seemed pretty scary. The Fremont Troll is one of the more famous outdoor sculptures in the area. He's pretty impressive, this shaggy-haired troll who seems to be crawling out of a cave under the bridge. He's massive, but all you can really see is his craggy face and his enormous hands, one of which is crushing a real, honest-to-goodness Volkswagen Beetle. Not a replica of a Beetle, but a real car. When we were little, Lily and I used to dare each other to walk on the troll's arm or touch his nose. Lily was right, though. He is kind of cute now, if you like the idea of a creature crushing a car.

"Yo, Elvis! Over here!" Ben called from the other side of the troll's hulking left arm.

"Who's his little pal?" Lily asked.

She wasn't talking about Scooter. Because walking on a leash next to Scooter was a little dog.

I was pretty sure the little pal was Daphne.

Chapter 20

"Is this . . . ?" I started to ask.

"Absolutely. It's Daphne. My grandfather asked me to take her for a walk. I'm Ben, by the way," he said to Lily.

"I'm the sidekick, also known as Lily."

"How in the world did your grandfather end up with Daphne?" I asked.

"I'm not exactly sure. But like I told you, Grandpa knows everybody. I think Jennifer asked him to keep an eye on Daphne while she went back to work."

"What did you find out about Daphne? How did Jennifer get her back? Where was she? What's the story?"

"I don't know exactly. All I know is that Jennifer said she didn't know what would have happened if she hadn't been able to come up with the same reward money as Ted," Ben said.

Yeah, the money that I saw her give to Mack last night, I thought bitterly. But I didn't want to say anything about the case until I had more evidence. So all I said was, "You didn't ask?"

"Uh-oh," Lily said under her breath. "When you hang out with Hannah, it's pretty much understood that you have to constantly assist with her cases."

"Cases? What are you talking about?" Ben asked.

"There's obviously a connection between the way the two dogs disappeared. Maybe there's a connection in the way they were returned," I said, talking a mile a minute. "But we don't know that because no one is giving us any details on who returned the dogs or how they were returned."

We walked back down the hill, with the three dogs leading us to their favorite water dish in front of The Perfect Pet.

"Maybe my grandfather knows what happened. I bet he can tell us something," Ben said.

We let the dogs finish their drinks, and then Ben started to lead Scooter down the street. "Let's go over to Costas Opa," Ben said.

"Is it time for a lunch break?" Lily joked. "Maybe we should go to Norm's so we can bring the dogs with us." I had told Lily about how the restaurant actually encouraged dog owners to bring their furry friends in with them. I couldn't tell if she believed me, or if she was testing Ben to see if I'd made the whole thing up.

But Ben just laughed and shook his head. Before I could ask him why we were really going to Costas Opa, the door to the restaurant opened and Mack walked out.

"Benito, my boy! Why don't you walk an old man home?" he asked.

"Sure, Grandpa," Ben said.

Then Mack turned to us. "Nice to see you, girls," he said. Then, of course, he tipped his hat. He always does that. But this time I couldn't smile in response. I was too dumbfounded.

"What's wrong with you?" Lily asked. I was still staring as Ben, his grandfather, and the two dogs all walked back up Fremont Avenue.

"I didn't know that was his grandfather," I said, feeling incredibly stupid. Ben was always talking about how his grandpa knew everyone. I'd seen him at least twice with Mack. How clueless could I be?

"How clueless can you be?" Lily asked for me. "I can't believe you didn't know that."

"You mean you knew that Mack was Ben's grandfather?" I asked, a bit surprised.

"Of course not! How would I know that?" Lily said with an exasperated tone. "But you're a detective. You're supposed to notice details like family relationships. But that doesn't matter, does it?"

Lily was right. At least on one account. I *should* have realized it sooner. I couldn't believe that I hadn't made such an obvious connection.

But on the other hand, she was wrong. It *did* matter. How would Ben feel if his grandfather turned out to be a dognapper?

CHAPTER 21

BY FRIDAY I still hadn't picked up any of my old clients. Both Boris and Daphne were home. No other dogs were missing. Yet people were still skeptical about me and my ability to take care of their dogs. Mom kept telling me not to take it personally. It was natural for them to worry about their pets.

"They aren't accusing you of anything," Mom said. "But they might be worried that their pets will be more vulnerable if they're with someone else."

Someone like Mack? I thought bitterly. But even though I had some strong suspicions about him, I couldn't prove that he had done anything. And no one else seemed to be worried about him at all.

Archie was a loyal client. On Friday, Elvis and I picked him up and brought him to The Perfect Pet. This time I was solo. No Lily. No Ben.

"And how are Elvis and Archie today?" Mack asked when I ran into him outside the door. He bent down to pet each of the dogs. "I'm glad to see these two getting extra walks in the daytime. Not good for an animal to go all day without a walk. Not good for humans to go all day without a walk, either." He tipped his hat and headed south on Fremont. I watched as he headed toward the canal. I had a pretty good idea that he was going to Costas Opa.

"Is Meredith working today?" I asked as I walked into The Perfect Pet. Arlene, the owner, was at the counter, and her poodle, who I'd learned was actually named Cinnamon, lay on a small mat on the floor next to her.

"She called in sick today," Arlene said, with obvious irritation in her voice. "Terrible time to be short staffed. Fridays are always busy. But we can always squeeze in nail trims for these dignified gentlemen."

"Only for Archie, the bulldog. Meredith just trimmed Elvis's nails."

I helped lift Archie onto the table. Arlene talked to him gently the whole time, telling him what a good boy he was. I helped distract him when she was working on his front paws.

"I hope Meredith is better tomorrow. We both volunteer at Elliott Bay Animal Shelter on weekends," I said. I'd missed last weekend and was looking forward to working at the shelter again.

"Sure, Meredith calls in sick to work, but she'll go off and donate her time to homeless animals," Arlene said.

I could tell she was more than a little ticked off. I decided to use the agreement technique to get her talking more. "It must be so hard to run a business under the best circumstances, but extraordinarily hard when an employee is sick."

"It sure is hard," Arlene agreed. "It's even hard sometimes when she is here. Nothing's wrong with Meredith's work, but her attitude is terrible. It seems like she's angry at the dog owners who live around here. And lately she's been acting as if she doesn't even need a paying job."

Arlene's last comment made me think. I knew Meredith didn't get paid for her work at the shelter. So if she was acting like she didn't need to get paid at The Perfect Pet, that could mean that she was getting money from somewhere else.

Arlene's voice interrupted my thoughts. "Okay, Archie. You're ready to dance away the weekend."

I helped Archie down, and we went outside, where Elvis immediately started barking. At what, I don't know. Have I mentioned that when a basset hound barks, it's extremely loud? Once Elvis got going for a while, he'd lift his head to the sky and start howling.

People called it a basset bray, but it sure sounded like a howl to me.

"Hannah!" Elvis stopped howling when Ben called my name. I wasn't used to seeing him without Scooter by his side. Elvis and Archie seemed disappointed.

"Where's Scooter?"

"I can't find him." Ben looked seriously distressed.

"Oh, no! Was he stolen?" Scooter was adorable, but he didn't fit the profile of the little cute dogs that had been snatched in the past week.

"I, I don't know. I've looked all over for him, but I can't find him anywhere. Can I use your cell phone to call my grandfather?"

I tried not to eavesdrop as Ben filled Mack in on the situation. Then Ben handed the phone back to me, saying, "My grandfather wants me to come home so we can figure out what to do. Can you come? Maybe you can help make flyers or something."

I told Ben I'd need to call my mom and ask for permission. She wanted details, like she always did: address, phone number, and all that. I handed the phone to Ben and he rattled off a bunch of numbers. Mom said she'd let Nikki know that I was keeping Archie for a while longer.

Ben and I practically raced up the street. Then up another. We were going up the steep hill and onto the street where that eccentric old guy is supposed to live. The wind kicked up a few notches, and the tree branches started whipping around. It made the huge beautiful house look old and creepy, just like a movie.

"You live here?" I asked Ben, amazed. He was opening the massive iron gate at the front of the property.

"In the back," Ben answered. "Come on."

My mind whizzed. First, I hadn't realized that Mack was Ben's grandpa. Now it turns out that Ben lived behind the mansion. Did that mean he knew the eccentric rich guy?

I followed Ben to the back of the house. Stone paths meandered through the back of the property, passing a fountain and a pond. Potted plants lined the edges of a stone patio. I had expected to see a smaller house in the back, but Ben opened a screen door and then a heavy wood door that led inside the mansion. He headed up an inside staircase to the right.

"This is where you live?" I knew there were important things to discuss, but I was in a temporary state of shock. We'd entered a light-filled room that stretched from the back of the house to the front. On one end, two large couches faced each other on either side of a stone fireplace. Another corner had two oversized chairs and ottomans, surrounded by books. Through an arched doorway was a formal dining room, the kind I've seen only in movies and on TV. The kind where you could easily seat twenty people for dinner and then the butler and the maid would come in and serve you a five-course meal. "You live *here*?" I asked again.

"Just the upstairs part. Grandpa had it converted when we came to live here. Dad and I live on this floor. Grandpa has the first floor, but he spends most of his time up here with me and Dad. Come on."

"Is it okay for the dogs to come?" I asked.

"Of course it's okay. Hurry."

Elvis had bolted up the stairs. Archie followed along as

well, but he needed some coaxing.

The kitchen was large, but I could tell it wasn't fancy-schmancy. This looked like a kitchen where people really cooked and talked and ate. Mack was at the stove, but he turned around when we walked in.

"Sit down and have some cocoa. And then we'll figure out what we need to do," Mack said.

"Grandpa, can I go back out? I want to keep looking around for Scooter," Ben said. "You and Hannah can decide what to put on the flyers." His grandfather gave him a hug and wished him good luck.

"Maybe I should go, too," I said. I wasn't so sure that I wanted to be alone with Mack.

But Mack stopped me. "Please stay," he said. His voice was so gentle and so full of concern for Ben that all my worries went out the window. How could I ever have thought that Mack had anything to do with the dognappings?

"I have some things I want to tell you. But first, I have a feeling you might have some questions for me, Hannah, so please feel free to ask. But don't let your cocoa get cold."

Boy, did I ever have some things to ask. As is often the case, my mouth got ahead of my manners. "I thought a crazy old guy with a bunch of cats lived here," I blurted out.

Mack laughed. "I'm crazy and I'm old, and my wife and I used to have many, many cats. I still have five. They're probably hiding from Archie and Elvis. My cats and I live on the first floor. My wife was terribly allergic to dogs, so we made this floor Scooter's floor. It is also Ben's floor and my son-in-law, Thomas's, floor. Ben's mother, my daughter, died three years ago. We wanted to do anything we could to keep Benito close to us. That's why we remodeled this floor to be their living quarters."

I was in awe that Ben had a place like this to live in, but when I learned that his mother was dead, I didn't feel like he was so lucky.

"And Ben's grandmother?" I asked.

"My wife, Brenda. She died of breast cancer last summer."

"I am truly sorry," I said.

"Benito's been through so much in his life. I don't want him to have to worry about Scooter," Mack said, thumping his fist on the table. It hit so hard it startled the dogs—and me.

"If you give me the information, I can go home and make a flyer right away. I already drew a couple of pictures of Scooter," I said. Ben had let me do a couple of sketches for my school art project. I had promised he could have the best one when my project was done.

"I don't think a flyer will be necessary this time," Mack said.

"Why? Has something already happened to Scooter?"

"No, no. I don't think anything is going to happen to him, although I'm sure he'd rather be home," Mack said. "The dognapper has already called and made a ransom demand."

"Oh, no. For how much?"

"The amount isn't important. I have enough, as you might imagine. But he, or she, won't return Scooter until tomorrow," Mack said.

"He or she? But if the dognapper called, couldn't you tell if it was a man or a woman?" I asked.

"It doesn't seem important," Mack said.

"You have to tell Ben!" Now I was mad. "I can't believe you let him go searching for Scooter when you know Scooter will be returned tomorrow."

"I told you, I don't want Ben to worry. It's better if he thinks Scooter is lost. This way, I can get the money to the thief first, and make sure I can get Scooter back safely. When the time is right, and I'm sure that I've put an end to all of this, I will tell Benito," Mack said.

"All of this?" I asked. "Do you think the dognapper is the same person who took Boris and Daphne?"

I hesitated a moment, then asked the question I really wanted to ask. "Wasn't there a ransom demand for Daphne as well?"

Mack looked surprised. "A ransom for Daphne?" he asked. "What makes you say that? Jennifer offered a generous reward, and that helped bring Daphne home."

"When I saw you the other night, it looked like Jennifer was giving you ransom money."

Mack laughed, a warm full laugh. "Oh, my dear girl. I wasn't getting a ransom. I was *giving* Jennifer money so that she could match Ted's reward. She felt it was the only way that she would get Daphne back. And it seems she may have been right."

Mack sighed, and then went on. "I have no idea who is behind all this. The only thing that matters to me now is getting Scooter back home where he belongs."

I did have an idea who was behind it. Especially now that I was sure it wasn't Mack. I filled him in on my theory.

Mack instructed me to take Archie and Elvis home, and then go help Ben search for Scooter. He also said not to follow him.

I half listened to him. Ten minutes later, I found Ben walking up and down Fremont Avenue, calling Scooter's name. I told him that I'd check over on Thirty-sixth Street. Something in my gut was telling me that Mack was on his way to the Lenin statue.

On the way over there, I was silently willing Archie and Elvis to be quiet. Mostly Elvis. I guess dogs really are intuitive, because they were both perfectly quiet, they sat motionless when I stopped, and they walked easily beside me when I walked. They were the best dogs ever, and I promised myself I'd give them extra treats when we got home.

I neared the Lenin statue, and sure enough I spotted Mack. Did the dognapper know this was where Mack had met Jennifer? Or was it just the most obvious meeting place? I made sure that Mack couldn't see me, and I watched to see what would happen.

Usually on TV, the person who arrives with the ransom money is jittery, looking around nervously, and drawing all kinds of attention to himself. Not Mack. He calmly stood about six feet from the Lenin statue.

"Now!" someone called. Apparently it was the command Mack had expected. He took an envelope out of his coat pocket and held it up in his left hand. He kept it up there.

A knight on a unicycle pedaled soundlessly across the square, snatched the envelope, and continued around the corner.

I am not making this up. You can't make this kind of stuff up. I'd just seen Ben's grandfather make a handoff to a cycling knight while Lenin looked on.

As ridiculous as it seemed, the knight costume was the perfect disguise. People were always wearing wacky things in Fremont, so nobody would really take notice. And with the helmet covering most of the person's face, it was impossible to identify the individual. I couldn't even tell if it was a man or a woman.

I watched as Mack dialed a number on the cell phone. I hoped it was to tell Ben to come home. Scooter would be back tomorrow.

CHAPTER 22

ELVIS, WHO HAD been unusually quiet on Friday (despite the knight on a unicycle), was back to barking and howling the next morning in the backseat of our Honda. I was going in to the animal shelter early because we didn't have either a game or practice that weekend.

We pulled into the parking lot at the Elliott Bay Animal Shelter. The sheer excitement of being around so many dogs and cats must have inspired Elvis to howl. Or maybe it was the shiny silver Lexus convertible that pulled in next to us.

"Elvis, quiet!" Mom commanded him in a gentle voice. Amazingly, it worked. Until the driver got out of the Lexus. The dog went bonkers again when he saw it was Meredith. Meredith driving a new convertible? Either pet grooming paid better than I realized or my suspicions about Meredith were on target.

"Great car!" I said, hopping out of the Honda. It must be brand-new from the dealer, since it still had Seattle Lexus plates on it, and a license number on paper taped to the back window. "Do you mind if I let Elvis out to say hello?"

"I'd love to see Elvis!" Meredith said. She seemed in an extra-good mood.

We walked into the shelter together. "Are you feeling better today?" I asked.

"What?"

"I stopped by the shop yesterday with Archie and Elvis. Arlene said you were out sick," I said.

"I'm much, much better today. In fact, I feel great. It was just a twenty-four-hour thing."

"Meredith!" the receptionist gushed when we walked in. "I'm so happy you could come in today. The director is making a special trip down here to thank you personally."

"It's nothing," Meredith said, practically beaming.

"Hannah, I have some good news," Leonard said. I followed him back to a small office. He handed me an envelope. A snapshot fell out of the inside card when I opened it. A photo of Izzie with an adorable little girl hugging her.

"Izzie's new family loved the sketch you did of her. I told them about the great volunteer we had here who had such a strong connection to Izzie. They said they'd love to meet you and your mom," Leonard said. "If it's okay with your mom, I'd like to give your phone number to Izzie's new owners. They may want to invite you over or something."

"Thank you! That's great," I said.

I was on a roller coaster of emotions today. I woke up

worried about Scooter, then I worried about Izzie, and now I was happy about Izzie. I went back to worrying about Scooter.

"We have a new arrival this morning. Meredith found him and brought him in earlier. He's in great shape, and he's probably just lost, not abandoned, judging by how he looks and behaves. You can start today by spending some time with him," Leonard said. I followed him down to the kennels where the dogs are kept. "Here's the big guy."

"Scooter!" I was thrilled to see him, but totally surprised to see him at the shelter.

Scooter, on the other hand, just seemed thrilled. The shaggy dog leaped to attention, jumped so that his front legs were on my shoulders, and started licking my face.

CHAPTER 23

"HOW DID SCOOTER get here?"

"You know this dog?" Leonard asked.

"You bet I know him. I know his owners, too," I said.

"That's great, because he didn't have a collar or any identification tag or a pet license on him," he said. "So, tell me who to call."

I pulled out my cell phone and scrolled through the recently dialed calls to find Mack's cell phone number. I gave the number to Leonard, but there was no answer.

"I know! I can call my mom. She can go to their house and tell them that Scooter's here. Or maybe I can just have my mom come and pick him up."

"As much as I trust you and your mom, I'm not authorized to release this dog to anyone other than his owners," Leonard said. "Go ahead and call your mom, though, and see if she can contact Scooter's owners."

After all that had happened in the past three weeks, I appreciated how careful the shelter was about things like this.

I got my mom on the phone just as she was pulling into the parking garage under PCC and our apartment. "I'll run up to the house right now," she said. "Wait. I still have the phone number Ben gave me yesterday when you asked to go to his grandfather's house. You can call that number, but I'll still run up there so we make sure we get the good news to them."

I dialed the number for Ben's house, and Ben's dad answered.

"Yes!" his dad screamed into the phone when I told him where Scooter was. "Ben and I will be there as fast as we can. Probably in fifteen or twenty minutes." He hadn't completely hung up the phone when I heard his dad calling, "Ben! Scooter's back! We can go get him now!"

Leonard gave me permission to have Scooter hang out with me since he was only going to be there for fifteen more minutes. My volunteer assignment for the morning was to help get invitations ready for a fund-raising party. I'd rather do something to directly help an animal, but when you're a volunteer you end up doing all kinds of things to help the organization. I went to the supply closet, Scooter by my side, to get more envelopes.

"Meredith, look who's here! Remember Scooter?" I asked. I watched Meredith's face closely, trying to gauge her reaction to my seemingly innocent comment.

Scooter, the most mild-mannered dog in the world, actually growled.

"He must be a little skittish of me since his last grooming," Meredith said, laughing awkwardly. "He probably thinks I'm about to give him a bath or something."

"Here she is!" said a woman as she came through the front door. "Meredith, I've heard so much about you as a volunteer, and on top of everything you've done you're making such a magnanimous donation to us! Imagine, another eighty-five hundred dollars for our shelter! It's absolutely wonderful."

Had she said $8,500? I started adding something in my head, but Meredith's voice interrupted my calculations.

"The amount has increased," Meredith said quietly. Everyone waited expectantly. The envelope stuffers in the workroom probably needed more envelopes, but I waited, too. "It's now closer to thirteen thousand. It's twelve thousand seven hundred fifty dollars." The handful of people in the room broke into spontaneous applause. Scooter started barking, something I'd never heard him do before. He ran to the front door, where he could see Ben and his father.

"Thank you for all your kind words," Meredith was saying. "But it's really all my pleasure. If you'll excuse me now, I have some dogs to bathe." Everyone laughed.

Just as Meredith left the front area, Ben walked in. I can't imagine a dog or a guy being any happier than they were. Leonard came out with some paperwork for Ben's dad to sign.

"I don't know much about where Scooter was found, Mr. Campo," Leonard said. "Let me find our volunteer who brought him in, and she can give us the rest of the story."

A car in the parking lot kicked up gravel as it pulled away.

"I think she just left," I said.

"We can get details later. All that matters is that we have him back. Thank you so much for keeping him safe until we could get here," Ben's dad said, pumping Leonard's arm.

Leonard patted Scooter on the rump. "Stay out of trouble, big guy."

"I'm so happy he's back," Ben said. "But what happened to him is still a mystery."

"I think this mystery is about to end," I said. Then I went back to work.

CHAPTER 24

IF I THOUGHT $8,500 was an interesting number, I found the figure $12,750 extra intriguing. I jotted down some numbers after I finished putting five hundred invitations into five hundred envelopes.

Reward money for Boris: $4,250

Jennifer had had to match what Ted offered in order to get Daphne back safely.

Reward money for Daphne: $4,250

That brings us to the $8,500 mark. If Mack had to pay the same price for Scooter, that would bring the total to $12,750. The same amount Meredith had just donated to the Elliott Bay Animal Shelter.

A coincidence? I think not.

After lunch, Leonard assigned me to help Meredith with bathing the dogs. "She's back now," he said. I think he was giving me an extra reward with that assignment. What a fun job. And what perfect timing.

I waited until we had a seventy-five-pound black dog

named Newton in the washtub to bring anything up.

"Nice car you had this morning. Is it new?" I asked.

"Brand-new. I ran into some extra money," she said.

Curiouser and curiouser.

"That was an interesting amount of money you donated today," I said, in what I hoped was a friendly, conversational mode.

"Just happened to be what I had available," she said.

Uh-huh.

I decided to go for it, TV-detective style.

"Meredith, how did you figure out it was Mack who fronted the reward money for Daphne?" I asked, abruptly changing the subject. It was a technique to catch her off guard.

She dropped the nozzle. Water sprayed out toward me. Maybe this wasn't the best time to get the facts.

"What are you talking about? Do you mean Mack, the old guy who hangs out at Costas Opa?"

I sighed. "You can be straight with me. I know you collected the reward money for the missing dogs. The rewards for Boris and Daphne equal the amount the shelter thought you were donating. But once you demanded that Mack match the reward price of the other two dogs, you upped it to that interesting figure of twelve thousand seven hundred fifty dollars. Not twelve thousand, or even twelve thousand five hundred. But twelve thousand seven hundred fifty. Exactly three times the amount of the original reward money, equal to the reward money for three dogs."

If only Lily could see me now. I was in acting mode, playing the part of a confident detective who has all the loose ends tied up. Truth is, I was still guessing on most of it. It'd be pretty embarrassing if I was wrong.

I didn't think I was wrong, though. Meredith's face was flushed red, and her jaw was set tight. I continued: "I don't know why or how you kidnapped those dogs. But I know that you were the one who got the money for them. And I think you're scrubbing this dog too hard."

She eased up a bit on the scrubbing. I didn't ease up.

"Once you made easy money with Boris, you just kept going. I just don't know how you figured out that Mack had something to do with Jennifer's reward."

She didn't say anything.

"I don't even know who to call to turn you in," I said. "Most of all, I don't know why you would do such a thing. If you love animals so much, why would you rip them from their safe homes and loving families?"

She helped Newton out of the tub. I handed her a couple of towels, and she started drying him. "People don't deserve the animals they have," she muttered. "I would never hurt an animal. I borrowed those little dogs only to make a point. The reward money for Boris was a nice surprise."

"You might have treated the dogs kindly, but their

owners were out of their minds with worry about them," I said. "Ted, Jennifer, and Ben love their dogs deeply. They take good care of them."

She didn't say anything. I had one last thing to say.

"Meredith, I've made up my mind. I'm not going to turn you in," I said. She looked relieved. "You're going to turn yourself in."

I know I have no power to make Meredith do anything. I'm not even very threatening. Still, I was pretty sure she was going to do the right thing.

"What makes you think she'll admit it all?" Mom asked as we drove home late that afternoon.

"Mack's going to help me with that," I said. "You'll see."

CHAPTER 25

BEN'S FAMILY INVITED my family to dinner that night.

"My grandpa is going to order a bunch of Indian food from Tandoor," he said when he called. "Dad says to bring Elvis, too. We've got some raw bones to keep the dogs occupied and out of trouble."

At seven o'clock, Mom, Elvis, Lily (she seems like family), and I entered the gate to the Mack Pappas, Thomas Campo, and Benito Campo yard. I wasn't sure if we were supposed to go around to the back and upstairs to where Ben and his dad lived, or ring the front doorbell. As if in answer to my unasked question, the front door swung open and Scooter came bounding out. Mack stood at the doorway. "Welcome, welcome! Come in. The food just arrived, and we're just setting up."

The first floor of the house was even more magnificent than upstairs. I didn't get much time to ogle because Mack ushered us back toward the kitchen. You could tell that this part of the house is where people actually lived. The kitchen opened to a comfy area for reading, watching television, and hanging out.

We helped set up a buffet with the takeout containers of Indian food. I piled my plate with vegetable *pakora*, eggplant *bharta*, and the most delicious spinach *nan* (yummy flatbread) I've ever tasted. We squeezed around the dining-room table, with Elvis and Scooter just feet away gnawing on their bones.

"Is it all set up now?" I asked Mack.

"Yes. As soon as we have the word that Meredith has contacted the police on her own, I'll make a donation of twenty-five thousand dollars to the Elliott Bay Animal Shelter," Mack said.

"So that's how you did it," Mom said quietly, squeezing my hand. I could tell by the tone of her voice that she was pleased with my plan and how it was shaping up.

"Wasn't the money Meredith was donating yours to start with?" Lily asked Mack.

"Just the money for Daphne and Scooter. Ted used his savings to be sure he'd get Boris back. But it doesn't matter where the money came from: it wasn't Meredith's to give away."

"How did she figure out you were the benefactor behind Jennifer's reward?" Lily asked.

"I don't know. Maybe she figured it out the same way Hannah did," Mack said.

Everyone looked at me. I tipped an imaginary hat on my head.

"How about that car she was driving this morning? Has she been doing this for a while and banking most of the money for herself?" Mom asked.

"I think I can answer that one," Ben's dad said. It turned out that Tom Campo was a private investigator. He had done some digging around and had found that Meredith had a $4 million trust fund.

"Wow," Lily said.

"I know. It's a lot of money," Tom agreed.

"No, not that. I meant 'wow' that you're a private eye," she said.

"Seems like I'm not the only detective around here," he said, winking at me. "I may, however, be the only licensed private detective at the table tonight."

One of Tom's friends at the police station was going to let him know when Meredith had held up her end of the bargain and admitted what she had done. As soon as that happened, Mack was going to write the check for the donation. Meredith had already returned Ted's money to him.

"I've already drafted the letter to go with it," Mack said, holding up a business letter. "It outlines how this money is donated in loving memory of Elizabeth Pappas Campo and Brenda MacMillan Pappas."

"Thanks, Mack," Tom said. He seemed a little choked up.

Ben got up and went around the table to give Mack a big hug. "Thank you, Grandpa. Thank you for making sure that Scooter—and all of the other dogs around here—will be safe."

CHAPTER 26

OUR FOURTH WEEK in Fremont was much more relaxed. So was the second month. My dog-walking business had picked up again, but I didn't take on as many canine clients as I had earlier. I decided I needed more time to draw and read and play Frisbee.

A few Saturdays later, Mom picked me up at three o'clock after my volunteer job at the animal shelter. "I have a surprise for you," she said. I looked in the backseat, but all I saw was Elvis and an empty water bottle.

"Tell me. Please."

"We're going to see Izzie," Mom said.

"Izzie the dog? Now? Really? How?" I was so excited!

"I got a call from Libby and Calvin, the couple who adopted Izzie. Leonard had already told them about you, and they wanted to make sure you didn't lose contact with her. They invited us to come over today because it's such a nice day. They thought Elvis and Izzie could meet each other and play outside," Mom said.

"I bet Elvis will love romping around without a leash on, won't you?" I scratched him behind his ears.

We drove across town to Capitol Hill. Mom parked just down the street from a park in front of a huge brick house.

Izzie sat on the front steps, looking at me for a few seconds. Then she lunged toward me. I hugged her like I never wanted to let her go.

"Do you know my dog?" a little girl asked.

"Is Izzie your dog?"

"Yes, Izzie is." She giggled and kept repeating "Izzie is, Izzie is."

"I'm Libby." A woman crossed the yard toward us. "You must be Hannah and Maggie. You've already met Rachel. And of course you know Izzie."

I was in heaven. Elvis was pretty happy, too. Libby invited us to the backyard, which was fenced in, so Elvis could, indeed, run free. I played with the dogs and with Rachel, who turned out to be darn cute and funny for a four-year-old. I'd tuned out the grown-ups' conversation, until I heard Libby say, "Maggie, I didn't know you were house sitters. How very interesting. I have someone I'd love you to meet." Libby asked if I'd watch Rachel while she took Mom next door to meet the neighbors.

Later, as we settled into the car, I asked, "What was all that about? You know, going next-door and all?"

"Their next door neighbors are going to Switzerland

for a couple of months. Some kind of business trip. It just might be a house-sitting opportunity for us," Mom said. "We'll see."

"Could anything be more perfect?" I asked. "You and me living next door to Izzie. Living in the big house. It's just too perfect."

Elvis moaned a little. "Of course, living with Elvis in Fremont is going to be hard to top," I said.

Elvis put his drool-covered chin on my shoulder, and we headed back to our temporary home, the Center of the Universe.

BOOK TWO

HANNAH WEST

on

MILLIONAIRE'S ROW

CHAPTER 1

SOMEHOW I MANAGED to get out of most of the hard work the last two times we moved. Not this time. Neither did my best friend, Lily.

"I thought you and your mom were minimalists," Lily said, her voice a bit muffled as she struggled with an armload of blankets and a down quilt. "Free of possessions and all of that."

"I'm a collector now. I need room for my works of art and my bric-a-brac," I said, trying to sound haughty. I was, after all, moving into a house on Millionaire's Row. And at that exact moment I tripped.

Lily giggled.

"You'd trip, too, if you were walking sideways with a masterpiece like this," I said, thankful that I hadn't gone all the way down or damaged the corners of the three-foot-by-four-foot canvas I was toting up the walk to our new house. This massive masterpiece was a joint effort that my mom's friend Nina and I had been working on for months in Nina's downtown Seattle studio. We'd just finished it last week. I had to shuffle sideways instead of walking straight ahead because the painting was so huge.

I couldn't see Lily, my best friend in the whole entire world, but I could sense her eyes rolling at me.

"I remember the good old days when you'd boast about getting all your possessions into your car," she grumbled.

Lily was kidding, of course. I may have tried to make a joke about how everything Mom and I owned fit into our old Honda Civic, but those kinds of jokes really never turned out that funny. Technically, you could say that Mom and I are homeless. But we really aren't; we just don't have our own home. Things had been kind of rough financially for Mom the past couple of years, but then Mom had a great idea. After we lost our house, we started lining up jobs house-sitting. People go on vacations or long business trips, and they hire us to take care of their homes and their pets. We're lucky that it all works out for us. And Mom's lucky she has me, I keep telling her, because I'm the one who actually does the most to take care of the pets. She, in turn, reminds me that she knows how lucky she is.

So here I am, moving into a three-story house on Fourteenth Avenue East at the top of Capitol Hill in Seattle. I put the painting down in the foyer (that's what people in big houses call their entryways) and stepped back onto the porch to look down the tree-lined street. I'd read about the houses here being "stately," which, according to my dictionary, means "majestic; imposing in magnificence, elegance; dignified." That about wraps it up, although I'd add "old, huge, and gorgeous" to describe the houses I saw on both sides of Fourteenth. Lumber barons and other rich businesspeople in the early 1900s built their houses at the top of this steep hill overlooking downtown Seattle and Elliott Bay. The street quickly got the nickname Millionaire's Row. I wouldn't mind being a millionaire today, let alone in 1906. My mind started mulling over how to figure out what the equivalent of a million dollars back then would be to today's prices. It's times like these that I need to shut off my brain. I'd already spent several hours on the tenth floor of the Seattle Public Library downtown researching Capitol Hill and our new street.

I had a good feeling about this street and this job, especially when a woman across the street with short spiky hair waved to me. She was walking with a younger woman, and I assumed they were on their way to a yoga class. The younger woman had a long, thin tote—the kind that people use to carry their yoga mats—slung over her shoulder. The woman who waved was carrying a rolled-up purple yoga mat and a purple tote bag with a yin/yang symbol on it. She obviously had an excellent sense of sophistication and style. My purple T-shirt with the yin/yang symbol on it happened to be one of my personal favorites. I'm the kind of person who has a list of all-time favorite symbols, and yin/yang is consistently in my top three. You see it lots of places these days. It's a circular symbol, half black and half white, with a small dot of white on the black side, and a small dot of black on the white side. It's an ancient Chinese symbol that some people call the "tai chi tu." The yin and the yang represent two opposing, but equal, forces. Lots of people say it's male energy and female energy, but it's more complicated than that. I like what I know about the concept. I also like that it's something with deep Chinese symbolism that's become part of American culture. I like to think of myself the same way: I'm Chinese, and I'm sure I have deep Chinese symbolism pulsing through my veins, but my American mom adopted me, so now I'm also deeply immersed in American culture. Ah, who am I kidding? I just like the way the yin/yang symbol looks.

The women stopped so that the younger one could take off her apricot-colored hooded sweatshirt and tie it around her waist. Underneath, she had a lighter apricot-colored T-shirt that had a swirling design surrounding the word *om*. The yin/yang woman looked older than my mom (who is thirty-eight), but like someone my mom would be friends with. The om woman—whose long dark hair was in a thick braid that reached almost halfway down her back—looked like she was about ten years younger.

As they started off again, both women smiled pleasantly at me. The older woman (aka Yin/Yang Woman) called out "hello" and "welcome to the neighborhood" when she saw my mom.

"Looks like we scored a friendly neighborhood again," Mom said to me.

"We're kind of lucky that way," I said. We'd easily made friends with the neighbors at every house-sitting job we'd had.

Mom turned back to the car. "Two trips this time. We need to scale back," Mom said, winking at me and putting her arm around me. "Come on. Let's get our last few things out of the car."

"I'll just wait for you in the piano room," Lily called after us. That's right. Our house has a piano—and the piano has its own room. And that room has a curved outer wall with windows that look out onto the street. The piano is the only thing in the room, managing to show off just how stunning a Steinway grand piano can be. "The only thing cooler would be if it revolved," Lily had commented earlier.

Mom and I headed back to our Honda while Lily hammered out "Chopsticks."

I grabbed my favorite photographs and some more artwork out of the car, along with my two goldfish.

"The cats are looking at Vincent and Pollock with a little too much interest," I said, trying to shield my goldfish from the all-knowing eyes of Simon and Sport, the two cats watching us from the porch.

"You'll have to keep the bowl covered so that all the cats can't go fishing," Mom said. When she said "all the cats," she wasn't just talking about the two outside watching us now. This house was home to Reba, Dolly, and Jasmine, as well as Sport and Simon. That's five, count 'em—five, cats.

"It's going to be different not having a dog around all the time," I said. Our last few house-sitting gigs involved dog-sitting and some dog-walking in addition to house-sitting. As a result, I've built a fairly successful dog-walking business with plenty of referrals. But I liked the idea of getting to hang out with cats for a change. Every time I spend the night at my grandma's house, her cat, Smiley, sleeps on my pillow, snuggled up to the back of my neck. Maybe I could get all five cats to sleep with me.

I knew I'd still get a lot of canine time. We were staying next door to one of my favorite dogs in the world, Izzie. I met her several months ago at the Elliott Bay Animal Shelter. I volunteer there a couple times a month, and I was there the day that someone brought Izzie in. She had been horribly neglected. We cleaned her up and nursed her back to health. I got extremely attached to her over the several weeks she was at the shelter. Luckily, she was adopted by Libby and Calvin. Even more luckily, my supervisor at the shelter had told Izzie's new family how she and I had a strong connection. Libby and Calvin invited Mom and me over to their house to see how well Izzie was doing. That's when Mom heard about the Parkers' trip and that they were looking for house sitters. And that's the happy story of how we ended up on Millionaire's Row.

"Maggie! Hannah! Welcome to the neighborhood!" Calvin, our new next-door neighbor and Izzie's new owner, pulled up in his black Mini Cooper. I couldn't see who else was in the car, but I could guess from the enthusiastic barks coming from the backseat. Calvin opened the car door and Izzie came bounding out. She rushed over to us, but used her good manners and sat expectantly, waiting for us to pet her.

"I missed you so much, girl!" I said, crouching down to give Izzie the attention she deserved. It had been only a week since I'd seen her last. Calvin and Libby also had a little girl named Rachel. They'd hired me to babysit her a few times, usually just for an hour or two as a way to break me in and train me. Libby said she was especially pleased that I had taken the babysitting class at Children's Hospital. We'd learned CPR, tips on safety, and ideas for keeping children entertained. I'd set up my own Babysitting Suitcase, full of art supplies, two lion puppets, a few little wood trains, and some of my favorite books. It was a modest assortment that paled in comparison to the books and toys lots of kids have. But the four or five kids I've babysat seemed superexcited to open what I called the "Special Day Suitcase."

"Libby and Rachel will be home soon," Calvin said. "Rachel is so excited to have you living next door. She asks every morning if it's finally the day when you're moving in so you can babysit her more often."

"I can't wait to babysit Rachel again!" I said. "I know we're right next door," I said to Calvin, "but here's my card so you guys have my cell phone number."

Hannah J. West

Pet Sitter, Dog Walker,
Plant Waterer, Babysitter, and
all around Errand Girl

235-6628

I added "babysitter" to my card just last week, now that I had official experience and a few references.

"We're going to go for a walk soon, before another rain shower hits," Mom said. "I'm sure Hannah would love to take Izzie with us on our walk."

At the first mention of "walk," Izzie sat down and looked at Mom patiently, showing what a good girl she would be. The second time Mom said "walk," Izzie barked. Dogs are amazing that way. I've never met a dog who couldn't pick that word out of an ordinary conversation. Even on TV. The dogs I know will be lounging around, maybe even seeming sound asleep, while the weather forecaster talks about Doppler radar, wind chill, El Niño, record highs and lows, overcast skies, sun breaks, and chance of rain showers (we have crazy weather here in Seattle, so you might actually hear all that in one forecast). Then the weather person throws in, "Take an umbrella on your walk" or "Good time to walk your dog." In a split second, the lounging dog will be up off its pillow and heading to the front door. Some dogs I know, including a labradoodle named Mango, even grab their leashes off hooks, generously assisting you while also getting out the door faster.

"I need to put my fish away, but then could I come get Izzie for our w-a-l-k?" I asked, spelling out the word. Izzie still barked. (And they say dogs can't spell.) Dogs are amazing, I tell you. "I'll see you soon," I said, giving her a good scratch behind her right ear.

We told Calvin we'd come by and pick Izzie up in about twenty minutes. Mom and I needed some time to explore our house. Who am I kidding? We needed time to explore our mansion. After all, we're living on Millionaire's Row.

CHAPTER 2

I RAN INSIDE to put my things down and to put Vincent and Pollock into their bowl. It was going to be a challenge finding a place that the cats couldn't reach. I dragged a kitchen bar stool over to the refrigerator, climbed up, and carefully placed the fishbowl on top. I gave an admiring glance to the refrigerator. It was one of those ones they call side by side, with the refrigerator on the right and the freezer on the left. Lily's family had one just like it. You could get crushed ice, cubed ice, slivered ice, and cold filtered water without opening the freezer door. Being able to get crushed ice with the push of a button never gets old to me. The rest of the kitchen was pretty amazing, too. Gleaming black granite countertops contrasted with bright white cabinets. Everything was sleek and polished. The kitchen looked like a showroom, mostly because there wasn't anything on the counters. Not even a toaster. There were so many cabinets and pantries that all the appliances were hidden.

"It's not forever, guys," I said to my fish. "I'll figure out a better place tonight." Simon, a part Siamese cat, was staring at me, twitching his tail. The top of the fridge didn't seem so safe anymore. I grabbed two vases and began setting up a makeshift wall around the bowl to protect it. The vases were superheavy. Even if one of the cats did get up there, it wouldn't be able to get to the bowl.

"It looks like you're building a fortress for Vincent and Pollock," Lily said, handing me another vase.

"I am. It's temporary, but necessary. Izzie's home, and we're going to take her on a walk so we can check out the neighborhood before it rains." I hopped down from the stool. "Want to look around the house before we go?"

"Mom's picking me up any second," Lily said. "But I do want to see some of this monster house before she gets here. I know she's dying to see it, too, but we have to go get The Brother from a birthday party, so she'll have to wait." Lily was on a kick of calling her little brother, Zach, who is actually pretty cute and not completely annoying, The Brother or, sometimes, Oh Brother. I think Zach secretly liked it.

I was excited to act as a tour guide and show off this huge house to Lily. We started in the sunroom, which is kind of like a porch but it's all glassed in. It overlooked the street and also, Mom had told me, would catch the morning sun. The owners, Happy and Frank Parker, told us they liked to sit out there in the morning and drink coffee, read the newspaper, do crossword puzzles, and watch the world go by on the street below. A loveseat with deep, red cushions, two chairs, and a coffee table made it seem like the kind of place you could stretch out and really relax. I'd already scoped it out as one—just one—of the many great sketching and reading spots in the house.

The main floor of the house had a living room, dining room, kitchen, office, and, of course, the piano room. That might not sound that extraordinary (except how many houses have piano rooms?), but each room was truly spectacular, mostly because of the size, the twelve-foot-high ceilings, the wood trim, and the immense windows. We headed upstairs, a trip that was impressive on its own. The wood staircase and gleaming wood banister are the kind you see in movies when the beautiful girl in an evening gown descends the stairs to the admiring glances of the roomful of dignitaries and royalty below. Halfway up the stairs was another choice reading spot: a long—at least eight feet long—cushioned window seat that was an ideal lookout to the neighborhood.

I took Lily up another flight of stairs to the third floor.

"This floor is off limits to us," I said to Lily, trying to sound ominous and mysterious. But I couldn't sustain the act, so I just opened the door to a weight room and workout area. "If you go through that door, you get to Frank's home office. He's an import/export guy, whatever that is."

"Don't they trust you up here?" Lily asked, eyeing the treadmill, rowing machine, and rows of weights.

"I was just kidding. They said we could use the equipment. I think this used to be where the servants lived, a hundred years ago. Because"—I paused while I opened what looked to be a closet door—"this is a secret staircase. It goes back down to the second floor, and then to the kitchen. This way the servants could get up at the crack of dawn and scurry down to the kitchen to make breakfast." Lily followed me down a flight of stairs, where we opened two other doors until we got out to the second floor hallway.

There were five bedrooms on the second floor. Mom said I could have first dibs this time, since there were a couple of house-sitting jobs where I ended up sleeping on the couch. This Capitol Hill house had so many bedrooms that we could each take two, and still be able to keep the master bedroom untouched until Happy and Frank returned. You might expect me to take one of the smaller rooms and leave the most deluxe for my mom. But if you expect that, you'd be wrong.

"Here's my new pad!" I said, swinging the door open to a guest suite. That's right. Not just a guest bedroom—but a bona fide suite, complete with a bathroom, walk-in closet (makes you wonder how long they expected guests to stay in the old days), and a "conversation area" with a love seat and two chairs. The bathroom itself was bigger than most apartments. Not only were there two sinks, but there was a whirlpool bathtub with steps leading up to it, a separate six-foot by six-foot walk-in shower (the measurement was

Mom's guess when we toured earlier), and even the toilet had its own room. My bed was king-sized, with a thick mattress and so many fluffy quilts and pillows that there was a step leading up to it.

"Can you believe it?" I asked Lily.

"It's like you have your own apartment, minus the refrigerator," Lily said.

"No fridge, but there is an electric tea kettle and a Japanese tea set," I said. "Besides, Mom would never ever let me eat in a bedroom."

I showed Lily the three other bedrooms, and then gave her a quick peek into the master suite, which was, if you can believe it, bigger and better than my guest suite.

"Now this is the best part," I said, opening the last door in the hallway.

"There's more?" Lily asked. "I can't believe it."

I really had saved the best for last. At least it was the best in my opinion. In addition to five bedrooms, the second floor had an art studio. It wasn't huge, but it was absolutely perfect.

"Voilà!" I said, in my best attempt at sounding like a French artist. "And guess what? Happy said I can work in here!" This was my idea of heaven. An entire room devoted to sketching, painting, and creating whatever you wanted. The room was directly above the piano room on the first floor, which meant it had the same curved glass window overlooking the street. Did I mention the fireplace? It didn't look like they used it much. My first clue was that instead of a grate and firewood, the opening was filled with a statue of an elephant. A big cushy chair and ottoman sat next to the fireplace, with floor-to-ceiling bookcases on either side. Happy had her own art library, along with a couple of shelves of travel books. Yet another place for me to hang out, read, and sketch.

"Is that a painting one of the owners did?" Lily asked.

"Yep. This is Happy's studio. Most of the paintings in the house are hers," I said. "Mom is completely ecstatic to be living here. She loves Happy's work."

Lily examined the signature on the painting. "But that name looks like it starts with a 'J.'"

"Her real name is Josephine, but she's been called Happy since she was little. At least that's what she told me. She also said that I'm welcome to work up here and use her supplies. She showed me where everything was and how to take care of things here," I said. "Ouch! Why did you do that?"

Lily had pinched my right arm.

"I wanted you to be sure it wasn't a dream," she said. "Oops, there's my mom down in front. I know she wants to see all of this, so I guess I'll just have to come back to your mansion tomorrow," Lily said. "Ta-ta. That's what you rich folk say, right?"

"I think we prefer 'cheerio,'" I said, walking her down to the front door.

"What, ho!" Lily tried to get in the last word.

"I'd settle for 'later,'" I called after her.

It was time for Mom and me to go for our traditional Get-to-Know-the-Neighborhood Inaugural Walk. Luckily, it still wasn't raining. I ran downstairs to check on Vincent and Pollock again. I didn't think any of the cats could get through to them now.

A fluffy white cat sat demurely by the entrance to the sunroom. "We're all going to learn to get along, aren't we, Jasmine?" I said, petting her between her eyes.

Reba, Dolly, Simon, Sport, and Jasmine were all inside now. I glanced up at my goldfish again, even though I was pretty sure they were safe.

"They'd better be here when I get back," I called to the five cats, as Mom and I headed next door to pick up Izzie.

Chapter 3

With Izzie walking between us, Mom and I headed north on Fourteenth Avenue East toward Volunteer Park. Every house we walked by seemed to be more magnificent than the last, getting taller and bigger as we got closer to the park.

I'd been to Volunteer Park lots of times, but usually to go to the Seattle Asian Art Museum or on school field trips to the Conservatory. I hadn't really walked around before.

"Let's go to the top!" I said when we first entered the park and came to the old water tower. When I was little, I was convinced that Rapunzel had once lived at the top of this round red-brick tower. I still thought that when I was six and Mom held my hand as we walked up the 108 steps (she counted) that spiraled to an observation area at the top where you can see all of Seattle, from Lake Washington to Elliott Bay.

I love running up the stairs to the top, even if I do feel a little sick when I look down. "Oh, wait. We probably shouldn't go up with the dog."

Mom agreed and promised we'd have plenty of time to

check it out some other time. We got to the art museum, where two camel statues flank the entrance to the museum. They're the kind of statues you just can't resist: they need to be touched, patted, and, most of all, climbed on. I handed the dog leash to Mom and ran up the steps and hopped on the back of one of the camels. Two little kids ran up after me, and then screeched to a halt as their mom said, "Wait your turn." I remembered how much fun I'd had on the camels when I was younger. (Who am I kidding? I still have fun on the camels. I imagine I always will.) I cheerily gave up my seat between the humps.

We walked around the reservoir, then back up the hill to the Volunteer Park Conservatory, a Victorian glass house where they grow cacti, orchids, banana plants, giant bird-of-paradise, and all kinds of other exotic and tropical plants that simply wouldn't grow in Seattle without TLC and a greenhouse.

"Sometimes I sneak up here in February when I'm tired of the winter rain and the gray sky," Mom said. "It feels so good to go from damp cold into the tropical air inside, or into the cactus room, where it's eighty degrees."

"You should bring me with you more often," I said.

"I will, especially now that we're so close. I promise lots of trips to the art museum, the water tower, and the greenhouses," Mom said.

"Cool!" I cried out. But I wasn't responding to her offer.

I could see tombstones on the outer edge of the park.

"I didn't know there was a cemetery here!"

"You've been there lots of times," Mom pointed out. "That's the cemetery where Bruce Lee is buried." She was right. I had visited his grave before, but I didn't realize that it was so close to where we were house-sitting.

Bruce Lee was a Chinese American from Seattle who is possibly one of the most famous martial artists of all time. He created jeet kune do, which is kind of like kung fu.

"This is so incredibly cool! Did you even notice what T-shirt I'm wearing today?" I lifted my Chavez Ultimate hoodie (my sweatshirt from my ultimate Frisbee team at Cesar Chavez Middle School) to show Mom my T-shirt underneath. Chinese characters surrounded a red symbol on a white background. The loose translation is something like "using no way as way" or "having no limitation as limitation." It was the symbol that was used in jeet kune do.

I love Bruce Lee. He starred in a bunch of martial arts movies like *Fists of Fury* and *The Chinese Connection.* I've seen all his movies. I'm not a huge martial arts fan, but I like that Bruce Lee was one of the first famous Chinese people in America. I would like him even if I weren't Chinese American, but I think I especially like him because he and I are both from China.

"Another place we'll come back to when we don't have a dog with us," Mom said. "We'll bring flowers, too." Bruce Lee's grave always had lots of flowers. You could easily spot his burial site all the way across the cemetery because there were usually at least a couple of people there to honor him.

We took a walk past the cafés and shops on Fifteenth Avenue East and looped back to Millionaire's Row. We truly had it all living here: big house, beautiful park nearby, coffee shops just a block away, not to mention being within walking distance to Bruce Lee's grave.

Calvin's black Mini Cooper passed us, and Izzie started pulling on her leash, as if she was going to run after it. The car pulled over in front of their house. Calvin got out with a bag of groceries.

"Good girl, Izzie!" Calvin said, taking the leash from us. "Thanks for walking her." He shifted the grocery bag to his left arm and started fumbling to get his wallet out, as if he was going to pay me.

"It wasn't official dog-walking business," I said hurriedly.

"Izzie was our excuse for getting out and walking around the neighborhood," Mom added. "We like to get to know the area where we're house-sitting as soon as we can after we move in."

"We'll make sure you know the neighbors, too," Calvin said. "There's our Block Watch captain now."

A woman in a brown velour jogging suit headed toward us, her forehead wrinkled up as if she were mad. Or confused.

"Grace? Is everything all right?" Calvin asked her.

"I just got back from my walk and . . . and I think someone has broken into my house."

CHAPTER 4

"ARE YOU OKAY?"

"What was taken?"

"Have you called the police yet?"

Calvin, Mom, and I were all talking at once. I pulled out my cell phone just as Mom said, "Hannah, call the police."

"No!" the woman said.

Silence.

"No, please don't call the police! At least not yet. It's, it's . . ." Her voice trailed off.

"Grace, what is it? Do you think someone is still in the house?" Calvin asked.

"Has someone threatened you?" I added.

"No . . ." her voice trailed off again. "I don't think anyone is there. And nothing seems to be missing."

"How did the burglar get in? Is there any sign of forced entry? Broken glass, maybe a jimmied lock?" I asked. As usual, my mom turned and gave me that "Keep quiet!" glare.

"No. I can tell that no one forced his way into my house," Grace said.

"Or her," I said. And I got that glare from my mom again. "His or her. The burglar could be a female."

The woman smiled for the first time. "I think he—or she—wasn't really a burglar. I shouldn't have even said that someone broke in. That's too strong of a statement. More like someone . . . visited."

"You had a visitor? And nothing is gone?" I hoped my voice conveyed that what I really meant was: What the heck is the problem then? Mom gave me another glare.

This interrogation was driving me crazy. Why didn't this woman just come out and tell us what was wrong and why she thought someone had been in her house. This time I slowed myself down, with no intervention from Mom. This wasn't an interrogation. We hadn't even officially met this woman yet.

"I know it sounds insane, but I'm sure that someone was in the house because things look different," Grace said, talking to Calvin.

"Did someone leave something inside your house? Something icky?" I interjected. (You can't keep a good detective down when questions need answering.)

"Nothing's missing. There weren't any threats. It's so embarrassing, but I think someone came into my house and . . . and . . . cleaned it up."

"Cleaned your house? That sounds like the kind of burglar we could all use," Calvin said, starting to joke until he saw the look on Grace's face. "I'm sorry, Grace. I still think we should call the police. There was an intruder in your home. You, of all people, should know how important it is to report things. You tell us that all the time at our Block Watch meetings."

Grace agreed to let Calvin make the call to the police. She must be really committed to being Block Watch captain because she had the police precinct phone number memorized, so she didn't have to tie up 911 lines with a non-emergency call. I handed Calvin my phone just as Mom rushed into an introduction.

"I'm Maggie West, and this is my daughter, Hannah. We're house-sitting for Happy and Frank Parker," Mom said.

"And taking care of their cats," I added.

"That in itself is a big job! Imagine, five cats," Grace said. "It's nice to meet both of you, although I'm afraid this isn't the best way to welcome you to the neighborhood."

"It is an unusual way to meet our neighbors," I said.

Calvin ended the call and said the police would come to Grace's house within the next thirty minutes. "I'd wait with you, Grace, but I need to be downtown in a half hour."

"I know you don't know us yet, but I'd be happy to wait with you," Mom said. Grace looked relieved. It would be kind of creepy to go back into one of these huge houses knowing that an uninvited guest had just been there—and maybe still was there. Unfortunately, I sort of said that out loud.

"It's kind of creepy to go back into a big house right after a B and E. The intruder may even still be there," I said.

Once again, my mother glared at me.

But Grace laughed. "You certainly speak the lingo, talking about a breaking-and-entering offense. I'm sure everything is fine, but, just in case, I would certainly appreciate the company."

CHAPTER 5

GRACE LIVINGSTON LIVED down the block in a two-story white house with a wrap-around porch. The porch was like an outdoor living room, with big comfy-looking couches and chairs, a coffee table, a wrought iron and glass table for eating, a rocking chair, and a porch swing. It looked like the cover of one of those home decorating magazines.

Grace bent down and moved a potted plant a few inches. "I'm going to have to find a new place for my key," Grace said.

"You don't mean you hide a key outside?" Mom said. "Under a flowerpot?"

"Another embarrassing thing to add to my list." Grace sighed. "I'm afraid I do. Whenever my son comes home from college, he almost always manages to forget his key. We tried hiding an extra in one of those hollow rocks you can buy, the kind that have a secret place for a key and then are supposed to blend in with your other rocks. But twice the gardener moved it and I spent fifteen minutes on dark, rainy nights lifting up every rock trying to find the right one. I had hoped that my new hiding place was so clichéd that no one would think a Block Watch captain would do something so unsecured."

I noticed an ACE Security Watch sticker on the narrow window next to the front door. "What's that sticker mean?" I asked.

"Nothing. I canceled the security system two years ago," Grace said. "Nora, our cat, kept setting off the burglar alarm every time she came in and out of the kitchen cat door. I'd hoped leaving the sticker up might deter burglars."

The porch was immaculate, except for a tiny bit of dirt near a flowerpot. "Did the intruder knock over the flowerpot?" I asked.

"It was upright when I got here. But that's the first thing I noticed. It looks like it was moved just a few inches. I assumed I'd forgotten that I'd moved it before my walk, even though I don't remember doing anything like that."

We followed Grace through the front door. The inside of her house was similar to ours—I mean, the Parkers'—house. A grand staircase stretched up to a landing on the second floor, the dark wood gleaming and inviting a ride down the banister. She led us into the living room, which had two separate seating areas. It looked pretty tidy all right, but I guessed that if Grace had a gardener, she probably also had someone come and clean her house.

"Maybe we should make a list of what's different, Grace,"

Mom offered. "Take your time going around and see what you notice. Hannah and I can take notes."

Grace opened the drawer of an antique cabinet and took out two notepads and pens for us.

"I don't use this room much, so it never gets too messy. Yesterday was the day Dana came to clean, too," she started.

"Didn't you say it was cleaned up today?" I asked, confused because it now sounded like it had already been clean.

"I should have said tidied up. My house was clean, but things are . . . rearranged. Those two chairs used to be over there," she said, pointing. "That glass bowl was on the left side of the table. I'd left *The New Yorker* open to an article I was reading, but now it's stacked up with the other magazines. Oh! The magazines are in a different order."

"They're arranged by size," I said.

"And the stack itself is neater," Grace added. "Let's see. I'm sure this bowl of rocks and sea glass was on the side table next to the lamp. Oh! That's strange." She picked up a polished rock, about two inches long and one inch high. "This isn't mine." She held it out for us to see. The rock was black with a symbol etched into it. It looked like kanji, characters used in Chinese and Japanese. I quickly sketched the symbol. I'm studying Japanese at Cesar Chavez Middle School, and kanji is just one of three scripts used in Japanese. Each symbol means a specific word.

There are tens of thousands of kanji symbols in Japanese. This one looked familiar to me, but I might just be thinking that because I wanted it to look familiar.

"Maybe your son or someone added the stone as a gift earlier than today," I suggested.

"I don't think so. This is my collection of sea glass we've gathered together on the beach at Whidbey Island. We always made sure that this was only sea glass, not pebbles or rocks, no matter how pretty they were."

A quick succession of raps on the front door interrupted our conversation.

"Seattle Police. We got a call."

CHAPTER 6

MOM AND I stayed until the police had made a thorough search of Grace's house, inside and out. It takes a long time when your house is a gazillion square feet and, on top of that, it's more than one hundred years old, so it has all kinds of nooks and crannies for hiding. I listened to Grace give her statement to the two police officers, who, I noticed, weren't taking many notes. Neither one of them even wrote anything down when she told them about the mysterious rock appearance. They would have been more interested if something had disappeared, rather than appeared. But when you think about it, having something *appear* is much more mysterious and intriguing.

They gave her a lecture on safety and securing a house, and left a brochure behind called "Stay Safe at Home."

It was clear to me that this case was mine. It didn't seem likely that anyone else would believe a woman whose complaint was that her house was tidier and, on top of that, someone had left her a gift.

I wrote Mom's cell phone number on the back of one of

my business cards and handed it to Grace.

"Too bad I don't have any pets that need sitting. And my son is already a sophomore in college," she said. "Perhaps I'll have a few chores and errands for you." She thanked us for being such good neighbors, and we headed back across the street to our house.

"I can't believe how big these houses are," I said, looking at a three-story brick house—complete with turrets and second-floor balconies—two doors down from Grace's and directly across the street from Libby and Calvin. I noticed a familiar-looking metallic ACE Security Watch sticker in a corner of a window. I hoped those owners were better than Grace at using their alarm system.

After dinner that night, Mom checked through the whole house, making sure that every window was securely closed and that every exterior door was double locked. "None of this 'hiding a key under a flowerpot' business for us," she said, as she handed me my copy of the house key and gave me her standard lecture on being responsible for taking care of the house. This was our job, Mom reminded me, and our clients count on us to make sure their house, their belongings, and their animals stay safe.

We both jumped at the sound of a clunk in the kitchen.

"Meow!" Simon, the biggest of the five cats, announced that he was hungry. We went into the kitchen to make sure everything was okay.

"Simon makes quite a racket when he goes through that

cat door," I said. Mom was down on her hands and knees, presumably looking to see if the cat door posed any threat to our safety.

"I can't imagine anyone could get in here through that, could they?" she asked me.

"Nope," I said, picking up Reba in one arm and Dolly in the other and heading upstairs to my room. I was amazed that these two cats, named after country-western singers, were being so quiet and letting me hold them, especially at the same time.

I set my laptop on the desk in the bedroom. I pulled out the sketch I'd done of the symbol on the rock. I went to a kanji Web site and began searching for a match. I tried the word *peace*, but it wasn't a match. There are several thousand symbols used in kanji, but fewer than two thousand were used regularly. If it took all night, I would go through all two thousand. But first I'd try a translation site where I could type in English words and see the ideograms. I tried a few typical words that we Americans like to see in Eastern script: *earth*, *water*, *happiness*, *calm*, and, finally, *harmony*. "Ladies and gentlemen, we have a match," I said to the cats.

The symbol on the rock left for Grace Livingston was Japanese kanji for *harmony*. A stone with that inscription would be a nice sentiment and a kind gesture under normal circumstances. But not if the recipient didn't know how it got there.

I checked online and saw that Lily was online, too, so I opened a chat window.

"We might have a new case," I typed.

"What's with 'we'?"

"You and me. The ace team at solving crimes . . ."

"At solving crimes no one else cares about."

"Calling you now . . ." I typed and signed off.

"Too many words to type," I said when Lily answered the phone. I filled her in on what had happened with Grace Livingston.

"Creepy," Lily agreed. "But I read something about how forgetful adults are, and I'm not talking senior citizens and Alzheimer's. People in their forties and fifties are getting spacey. That's why there are all those infomercials on TV about boosting your brain power and improving your memory. I'm telling you, there's a memory crisis in America."

I wouldn't exactly call it a crisis, but I let Lily go on a bit while I double-checked the word *harmony* in different languages. I didn't really need to prove anything, but it was fun to compare and contrast the interpretations in style even within the same language.

"I'm still going to keep an eye on things. Grace seemed seriously spooked," I said.

Later that night, I woke up when Simon the cat jumped on my bed. "You're a big fat noisy guy," I said. I thought I heard something else. I tried to make my ears superaware so I'd hear anything out of the ordinary. Then again, I didn't know what was ordinary in this house yet. I tiptoed to the door and looked out in the hallway.

"It woke you up, too?" Mom whispered.

I screeched a little at the sound of her voice.

"Sorry. I didn't mean to startle you," she said. "It's just a creaky board on the third step." She demonstrated by putting her weight on and off the step. "Even a small cat like Jasmine sets it off."

"Okay, then..."

"Want to grab your blanket and sleep on the couch in my room?" Mom asked.

Sometimes I think my mom is a mind reader. This house was too big, and I wanted to be close to her.

Mom, me, and five cats all slept in the same room for the rest of the night.

CHAPTER 7

AFTER THAT FIRST night of scary noises (which weren't even that scary), Mom and I quickly got used to the house. It was pretty easy to enjoy living in such luxurious surroundings. This was quite possibly the cushiest job we'd ever had. While I was at school that week, someone came to mow the lawn, someone else came to clean the house, and a third person came to prune the bushes in the front. Not much for us to do but sit back and relax. And take care of five cats.

I think I earned my keep with those cats, however. Feeding them was no big deal, but cleaning out three litter boxes twice a day wasn't exactly my idea of a good time. I'd been running a little late Thursday morning before school, so I'd skipped the morning kitty-cleanup routine. I was dreading seeing what was waiting for me in the afternoon as I walked home from the bus stop after school.

The garbage and recycling trucks had made their way down our street earlier in the day. One of my regular jobs when we house-sit is to bring the garbage and recycling out to the curb first thing in the morning on garbage day. As soon as I got home from school, I wheeled the cans back to their spots. To potential burglars, empty garbage cans are like a beacon that no one's home.

This neighborhood was so nice that the waste-management people put the garbage cans upright and put the lids on after they emptied the garbage. On lots of other streets you see the empty cans strewn about, usually on their sides, and often rolling over the curb and into the street.

I unlocked the door to the house, called hello to the cats, put my things down in the entryway, called Mom at Wired (the coffee shop where she works) to tell her that I was home. She reminded me to put the trash can and recycling cart away behind the house.

"I'm already on it," I said. I went to the sidewalk and secured the lid on the brown garbage can, and started wheeling it to the back. I saw people at two houses across the street doing the same thing. One woman looked up, and I recognized her as the woman with the spiky hair who'd been carrying the yin/yang tote bag the other day. She smiled, waved, and began wheeling the recycling cart to the backyard. At the brick house next door to her, her friend with the apricot hooded sweatshirt was doing the same thing. She looked across the street, but she didn't seem to see me. The three of us made quite a cacophony (vocabulary word for the week) with our noisy, clunky wheels rolling on the pavement. I came back to get the green recycling container, which, luckily, was also on wheels. The apricot hoodie woman across the street was ahead of me, though. She already had the recycling can behind the fence and was closing the gate. I hoped to catch her eye so I could do the friendly, neighborly waving thing. But she didn't look up as she headed off toward Volunteer Park. The other woman must have gone back inside her house.

You know how sometimes what you don't see is what strikes you as odd? That's what happened. I headed back inside, then stopped and looked back across the street. Something was missing.

Garbage cans! On the east side of the street, the garbage and recycling cans were all put away. On our side, they were all (except for ours) still curbside.

It wouldn't make sense that everyone on the entire side of the street would already have moved their cans. Grace Livingston's house was on that side of the street, and I knew she was still at work at the University of Washington. She'd made a point of telling us she worked until five every day.

Then again, maybe Grace and her neighbors had hired someone to put things away during the day while they were at their jobs. These people hired out just about everything, so why not pay someone to wheel your trash cans away?

It was weird, but not criminal. I decided to be neighborly, and I took Libby and Calvin's cans down their driveway to the outside of their garage. Then I went inside to face the litter boxes.

CHAPTER 8

THAT NIGHT, during dinner, Mom got a phone call from Grace Livingston. She was calling an emergency Block Watch meeting.

"You're not going to believe this," Mom said. "Two of the brick houses across the street had intruders today."

"Was anything stolen?" I asked.

Mom shook her head no.

"Let me guess: things were cleaner than when they'd left in the morning?"

Mom nodded.

"Did they find any gifts, like rocks?" I asked.

"Grace asked both families to look around for that specifically. There were rocks at each house. But there was something else. At each house, there was something even odder left behind," Mom said. "You'll never guess."

Whenever someone says "you'll never guess," something inside of me takes over and I turn into a Guessing Machine.

"A million dollars . . . a big-screen TV . . . a new bicycle . . . a hamster . . . a pony . . . a piñata . . . fresh flowers . . ."

"Bingo!" Mom said. "Fresh flowers at one house. You're coming with me to the meeting to tell what you saw with the recycling. It might be nothing, but it might be significant. Then you'll get to hear firsthand what was left at the other house."

I brought my sketch pad with me to the Block Watch meeting, which was being held next door at Libby and Calvin's house. The adults gathered in the living room. I volunteered to take care of Rachel, partly because I really like her and partly because I wanted an excuse to be on the fringe of the meeting so I could observe everything. Rachel and I set up some crayons and a coloring book at the dining room table.

"What are you going to color?" she asked, concerned that there was only one coloring book, and it was clearly meant for her.

"I have my sketchbook. I almost always have a book like this with me," I said, showing her some of my drawings. "This way I can draw or color or write whenever I feel like it." I couldn't tell if she was impressed because she was already busily intent on her coloring work. Izzie came in and curled up on the floor by my feet. I started sketching random things I saw, beginning with a blue vase that had a silver cut-out pattern on it that made it look like irises were growing all around the vase.

"The police officer who came to the house didn't even bother writing anything down," one man in the living room said.

"It's still a crime to enter someone's house uninvited, but they don't seem too concerned."

"They'd rather wait until it's too late, either something is stolen or someone is hurt," a woman added.

Everyone started talking at once. Grace quieted them all down. "It looks like everyone's here, so let's get started."

"Should we wait for Louise?" someone asked.

"She called me right before I came to say that she didn't want to miss her yoga class. She said something that sounded like 'ash-tango,' whatever that means," a woman answered.

"We can fill her in later. Perhaps we could hear from the owners of the two homes that were 'visited' today," Grace said, directing her comments to four people on the sofa.

Both had the same M.O. as Grace's intruder: No sign of forced entry, nothing missing. Furniture was rearranged, and piles of books and magazines were tidied up.

"Hannah may have seen something odd this afternoon when she got home from school," I heard Mom say.

All heads turned toward me and Rachel in the dining room. I stood up and cleared my throat. I'm not the shy type, but talking to a roomful of adults is always a little intimidating. "It might not be a big deal, but when I got home from school, around three o'clock, I noticed that all the houses on the other side of the street already had their garbage cans put away. Things just seemed out of balance, because the cans were still out on this side."

"Tony must have brought ours in," one woman said, but her husband was already shaking his head no.

"I assumed you did it when you got home from work," the man said.

"It's probably not a big deal. It just struck me as odd," I said. I could feel my face heating up with embarrassment. My mom has all this confidence that because I'm a visual learner it means that I notice things that others might not. "Maybe your neighbor in the house with the turrets took care of it. I saw her and another woman when I got home from school."

A man and a woman on the couch interrupted: "That's our house!" they said at the same time.

"Oh, I don't really know who lives where yet," I said. "Maybe it was your daughter? Or a friend? It was a woman in an apricot hoodie." I had a feeling they might not all know what I meant, so I quickly added, "A sort of light-orange hooded sweatshirt. She has long dark hair."

The couple looked at each other and exchanged "Do you know who that is?" comments.

"Maybe she was just helping out the woman with the short spiky hair," I said. "She was outside, too."

"Oh, that's Louise," the woman said, visibly relieved. "She's always doing nice things for people. She has a crazy schedule, so she's often home during the day."

"That explains it! I think the woman I saw at your house is friends with Louise," I said. I was alternately relieved and disappointed: relieved that it wasn't something creepy going on, and disappointed that I hadn't discovered something useful for this case.

"I'm sure that explains it. Maybe Louise felt like being neighborly and returning all the garbage cans and she asked a friend to help. Louise is like that: extremely helpful and bighearted," Grace said.

Everyone started talking. Once again, Grace quieted everyone down. I think they all realized that it's kind of a silly thing to get all worked up about. Still, it was weird.

As long as I was embarrassing myself, I might as well keep going. "I have one other question, if you don't mind. Do you use ACE Security? I noticed a sticker at your house." I directed my question to the couple who owned the house with the turrets, one of the two homes that had been broken into earlier today.

"No, we've never used a security company. That sticker was there when we bought the house, and it was impossible to get off," the woman said.

"There's an ACE Security sticker on my front door, too," said the man who lived in the other house that had been broken into. "I've tried everything to get it off without damaging the wood."

Interesting.

"Most houses on this street used to have ACE Security," a man said. "They probably all have stickers."

I wasn't sure if he meant that to be reassuring or not, but everyone seemed to be nodding.

"Does anyone have an active account with ACE Security?" I asked. No one did. Doubly interesting. I made a note of it.

People had been passing around the stones that had been left at each of the three houses. When they got to Mom, she handed them to me with a meaningful look. I knew exactly what she meant. I placed them on the coffee table to compare them. Each one had a different symbol, but now that I'd researched the first one, I could see that all three stones had Japanese kanji. I copied the symbols into my sketchbook.

"Is there anything else that seemed amiss in your houses?" Calvin asked the neighborhood group.

"There's one thing," the woman from the brick turret house began. "It's just a little thing, but I'm sure the toilet lid in the foyer bathroom was open when I left for work this morning. It was closed when I got home."

"Maybe Charlie closed it on his way out," someone suggested.

Charlie shook his head. "I left before Jodi and got home after her. If she says she left it open, it was open. She does it on purpose."

That's kind of a weird thing to say.

"I leave it for the animals," she said, turning bright red.

"I'm not gross or anything. It's perfectly clean. We never use it as a toilet. I just have this fear that I'll be away from home and there will be an earthquake or some other disaster and I won't be able to get home to our dog and cat. This way I know they have water."

"That's weird," I said, not realizing I said it out loud at first. Then I was the one turning bright red. "I mean, it's not weird that you leave it open. It's weird that it was closed. It just seems like a totally odd thing to do, doesn't it?" My voice trailed off, but it didn't matter, because all the adults seemed to be talking at once. This gave me time to think things over. To me, it didn't seem at all unusual to keep a toilet lid open so their animals could have water. If anything, it was practical. We had the opposite instructions in our current house-sitting gig. We had to make sure all the toilet lids were closed. One of the cats, Sport, had a thing for water. His owners feared he'd dive into any water he could find and not be able to get out. It might be a crazy thought, but better to be safe, right?

I was lost in my own watery thoughts until I saw Jodi, my fellow animal lover, holding up four red squares, each about three inches by three inches. Everyone quieted down. Was this some weird meeting ritual, where a red card meant "stop and be quiet"?

Turns out the red cards had an even weirder meaning.

CHAPTER 9

"THEY LEFT A paint chip at the house?" Lily asked me at lunch the next day. We were standing in line to get our daily dose of burritos. People never believe me, but the burritos at our school are truly delicious. The school buys them from Trader Joe's, so they're actually the same kind of burritos most of us have at home anyway. There's just a stigma about school lunch food being bad. It turns out it doesn't have to be.

"Several paint chips," I said. The thief, or rather the *un*-thief, as Lily and I decided to call the culprit, had left paint sample cards—the kind you get in the paint aisle of the hardware store—in Jodi and Charlie's house.

"Maybe it was an accident and it fell out of a pocket or something," she said, grabbing a tiny bag of organic baby carrots. We headed for a long table where Jordan Walsh and some of our other friends were sitting. This was our best schedule ever, since we had first lunch, and it turned out that a bunch of our friends from elementary school had the same lunch. We sat together at the same table every day. After Jordan and I became friends, she started sitting with us, too. We spent most of our time trying to avoid making eye contact with eighth graders. Of course, next year we'd *be* eighth graders. We'd have to find something else to be insecure about.

"The un-thief is cleaning things up. It hardly seems like this type of person would make a mistake like that. Besides, these weren't random paint samples. They were all in the same color family. Plus," I said, pausing to emphasize my next statement, "they were taped to a wall."

I'd seen the paint chips, and they were all these deep shades of red. They had names like "Long Johns Red," "Cardinal," "Red Barn," "Firecracker," and "Heart-Pounding Red." Since our friends had heard part of our conversation, we all spent the rest of lunch thinking of paint names. (Siamese Kitten Brown, Bloody Gash Red, Poisonous Purple, Scabbed Knee Brown . . . you get the idea. Of course, Jordan had to throw in Crimson Lake, the color we had dubbed the red streaks in my hair.)

All of this color talk gave me an idea. I'd have to wait until I got home to check it out, though. The last three hours of the school day truly crawled by. A new house meant a new bus route, so right after seventh period I said good-bye to Lily and walked four blocks to the Metro bus stop on Martin Luther King Jr. Way. I waited for the Number 8 with Chandra and Ari, two eighth-grade girls from my gym class.

"We can wait for you by the lockers next time, and we can all walk here together," Ari said.

"Are you going to keep taking the 8?" Chandra asked.

I told them I'd be on the Number 8 for a few weeks. I like that they didn't ask questions, but maybe they didn't ask because they weren't that interested in a seventh grader. Still, I didn't want anyone to know that Mom and I didn't have a real home. And as much as I'd like to be rich, I didn't want anyone assuming that I really lived on Millionaire's Row. They got off the bus before my stop on Fifteenth.

As soon as I got home, I greeted the cats and checked on my goldfish. I'd moved Vincent and Pollock to a larger bowl with a custom-made metal screen over the top, thus protecting them from any kitty who might feel tempted to go fishing. Still, I'm a little paranoid about these two guys, so I checked on them several times a day. I think they appreciated the company.

It was Friday afternoon, and I had a couple of hours to myself before I went next door to babysit Rachel. I pulled out my sketchbook and looked at the symbols on the stones the un-thief had left in three different houses. I resketched them, just as a way to focus my mind. Drawing does that for me. Soon I was lost in drawing and shading things, until I really looked at what I'd done. In addition to the kanji characters, I'd shaded the page with different reds. I'd also drawn a diamond shape with the word *ACE* in capital letters inside it.

ACE! How could I have forgotten? A few online searches later, I decided to pull out the phone book and simply look up the company in the business listings. There were two columns of companies that had names starting with the word *Ace*, but none of those companies dealt with home security. I randomly picked a security company from the yellow pages. I felt like a classic detective from an old movie, looking for information in a phone book.

"Hello? I just bought a house on Capitol Hill," I said into the phone. I don't know why, but when I'm trying to sound like a grown-up on the phone, I stand up and begin pacing. "It used to have a burglar system, I mean an anti-theft system, and the sticker is still on the front door. I just hate having stickers, so I'd like to start service with that same company.

"No, it isn't your company. And I completely understand that this isn't something you would normally do, but I would be so appreciative if you could tell me how to get ahold of ACE Security Watch."

The reply wasn't quite what I'd expected. It didn't really matter since the people on Millionaire's Row didn't have active burglar systems. Apparently they wouldn't ever be active with ACE again. The company went out of business three years ago.

Maybe I'd have better luck looking at kanji. I picked up my sketch. The combination of the shades of red and the kanji reminded me of something . . . of something I'd seen recently. I closed my eyes and willed the original thing that had triggered my memory to pop back into my head. Sometimes it works, sometimes it doesn't.

This time it did.

I went to the reading area that Happy and Frank had set up in the sun porch. The coffee table held a stack of books. There it was: the second one down, a red spine with kanji. I pulled out *Feng Shui for Your Home* and paged through the book until I came to a photo of stones with ideograms. There they were: harmony, serenity, and simplicity. The same as the three stones left in our neighbors' houses. I turned to a chapter on color, skimming the type until the word *red* caught my eye.

"Red is an auspicious color. Consider using it on a south wall of an office or studio to increase creative energy and enhance prosperity."

I looked out the sun porch window to figure out which way was north and which way was south. Jodi and Charlie's house, the one with the turrets, faced west. Based on the way they'd described the scene, I was pretty sure that the red paint samples had been left on a south wall in the living room.

I flopped down on the bed to look through more of the book. Placement of flowers were discussed in another chapter. Still another had an extremely interesting passage:

"Career opportunities enter the home through the front

door. If a bathroom is located near the front entry, be sure to keep the toilet lid closed when not in use. Otherwise, your opportunities could flow away immediately. Chi and fortune can be literally flushed away."

As I read that, I was struck by an obvious realization.

Our un-thief was studying feng shui.

CHAPTER 10

I DON'T KNOW much about feng shui, except that it's a Chinese term and it refers to the theory that where you place things in a room helps determine the positive flow of energy. I went to my favorite online dictionary and found this:

> **feng shui: The Chinese art of positioning objects in buildings and other places based on the belief in positive and negative effects of the patterns of yin and yang and the flow of chi, the vital force or energy inherent in all things.**

According to the little bit I'd garnered from paging through the book, someone who practices feng shui would pay attention to color, balance, and placement of things including couches, mirrors, and a bowl with sea glass in it.

Now I just needed to find someone locally who practiced feng shui and had a way of getting into other people's houses. That's all.

It was almost five o'clock. Mom wasn't home yet, so I called to let her know that I was heading next door for my Friday-night babysitting job. She made me promise to call when I got there, too. It's so embarrassing. Then again, having to call to check in so often was a small price to pay for all the independence I had.

Libby opened the door and Izzie came running to meet me, with Rachel close behind. Izzie sat down and looked at me expectantly. In one swoop I knelt down to hug Rachel and pet Izzie.

"Where's the Special Day Suitcase?" Rachel asked. She said "special" so it sounded like "spess-ul." So cute.

"It's on the front steps. Do you think you could help me bring it in?"

Rachel didn't need to answer. She pushed past me to get outside and grabbed the suitcase handle, proudly wheeling in my babysitter suitcase o' stuff.

"We're going to have so much fun tonight!" I said as Rachel led me by the hand into the living room.

Libby was going downtown to meet Calvin after work. They were going out to dinner and to a play at the Fifth Avenue Theatre. "We should be home by eleven o'clock. Rachel's bedtime is eight o'clock. The pizza just came. Lots of root beer in the refrigerator," Libby rattled off as she bustled around the kitchen/family room getting her purse, her keys, and her jacket. She kissed her daughter good night and headed out.

"Let's eat pizza!" I said, gratefully noting that Libby had ordered from Pagliacci, my favorite pizza-delivery place. One half was plain cheese. The other was artichokes and mushrooms—my favorite! "How did your mom know what kind of pizza to get?"

"She called your mommy," Rachel said

This was a pretty sweet arrangement.

"Are you going to be in the parade tomorrow?" Rachel asked me.

"What parade?"

"The one that goes right down our street. The one that goes tomorrow. I'm going to be a firefighter in the parade," she said proudly. Could I love this girl any more? I've seen lots of four-year-old girls who are obsessed with being princesses. But not Rachel. She was a free-thinking preschooler who was going to some parade somewhere dressed as a firefighter. I couldn't think of any holiday or big celebration that would be happening that weekend. Maybe it was a neighborhood parade down on Broadway or up on Fifteenth.

After two games of Trouble and three hands of Go Fish, Rachel was ready for story time. Four times through *Skippyjon Jones* (featuring a Siamese cat who is convinced he's really a Chihuahua), and Rachel's eyes were starting to close. Izzie and I waited in her room until she was completely asleep, and then we quietly tiptoed downstairs.

"Ready to be my model again?" I asked the dog. I'd drawn Izzie several times when she was at the shelter. In fact, one of my drawings was in a frame on the wall here. She'd truly found the perfect home (especially since her new family appreciates fine art by *moi*). I got comfy on a couch in the family room and started sketching. My yearlong studio-art project at school was all about dogs. We did lots of other things throughout the year, but we were supposed to be working on one theme consistently during the year to see what kind of progress we made. The first drawings I'd done of Izzie focused on her and her alone. Maybe if I put some things from a family home into the picture I could signify that she now had a permanent place to live. I invited Izzie up onto the couch. I moved a photo of Rachel on the end table so that it was closer to Izzie. A vase on the end table would give some nice height.

"Wait a second," I said out loud. Izzie lifted her head slightly in case I said anything of interest to her. "This vase was in the dining room two nights ago." It looked good in its new position, but it also seemed a teensy bit dangerous to have this porcelain vase in a low, open area in a house with a rambunctious preschooler and a tail-wagging dog. When Libby had seen my sketch of it the other night, she'd told me how much she'd always loved that vase and how it had been her great-great-great-grandmother's.

I headed toward the dining room, with Izzie padding after me, to see if maybe there was another vase just like this one. But the vase I'd sketched on Thursday night was in the family room, not the dining room. A different vase, a bit taller, was in its place. I also noticed that the dining room table had been turned 90 degrees. The chairs were placed with two on each long side, instead of one on each of the four sides, as they had been the last time I was there. People rearrange their furniture all the time, but this felt strange. I couldn't tell if anything else was different. I scanned the hutch and the top of a dining buffet.

Next to a glass bowl of little oranges was a small black polished rock. I picked it up, already knowing what I was going to see. This time, I could even decipher the kanji. It was a character I'd seen several times while researching the other three stones.

This one said "energy."

CHAPTER 11

I DID WHAT any top-notch private eye does in a situation like this:

I called my mother.

I had imagined how creepy it would be to know that someone was inside your house. Someone you hadn't invited. And now I was feeling it.

Two hours later, Libby and Calvin pulled into the garage. They came in through the basement and up to the family room. "We're home!" Libby called. "All boyfriends up here with Hannah better disappear—" She stopped midsentence when she saw my mom. A look of panic instantly took over her face.

"Everything's okay!"

"Rachel's fine!"

Both Mom and I started talking at the same time, knowing that Libby and Calvin would be obviously worried why their responsible babysitter had needed her mother to hang out with her. I could tell they still felt something was wrong, even after they checked on Rachel and kissed her while she was dreaming.

Libby came back to the kitchen and offered us tea. She has one of those contraptions in which you heat water in the morning and it stays the perfect temperature for tea all day. I'd seen this same thing at Uwajimaya, a Japanese market down in the International District/Chinatown. (People between the ages of forty and sixty tend to call that area the International District, which is what it was called in the 1980s. But it's really Chinatown, so now people do a slash when they talk about it. You know: a slash in the middle so that it's both things: International District/Chinatown.)

"Did you move the water, Hannah? It's absolutely no big deal if you did. It must have been heavy to move, though," Libby said.

"Nooooo, I didn't move it," I said.

"That's strange. I guess Calvin did this morning, and I was so busy all day I didn't even notice. Although I did make tea this afternoon . . ." Her voice trailed off.

"Where is it usually?" I asked while I grabbed my sketch pad. I added "water contraption moved" to my list of odd occurrences.

"It's in the corner, between the wall and the toaster," she said. She was looking at the vase on the end table. Her face was scrunched up in a look I interpreted as puzzled.

I looked at Mom. She nodded to me, a signal to go ahead. I took a deep breath.

"I don't know your house that well yet, but I was wondering about some other things that have been moved since we had that meeting last night," I said.

Libby plopped down on the sofa. Calvin, who had gone upstairs to change out of his suit and into sweatpants and a T-shirt, sat next to her and asked, "What's wrong?"

"Someone's been in our house. That's what you think, isn't it? Oh, dear! Was it tonight, while you and Rachel were alone?"

I didn't think it had happened while we were there. You'd think I'd pick up on it if someone had been moving furniture around in the dining room.

"I don't think so," I told her. "I was drawing Izzie tonight, and I noticed that vase was in the family room. I noticed only because I had sketched the vase last night when it was in the center of the dining room table," I said.

"Those pictures, the photographs," Calvin said. "Those were in the dining room, too, weren't they, Lib?"

Mom and I followed them into the dining room. "I don't suppose you and Rachel were rearranging furniture tonight?" Libby asked softly. I shook my head no.

"There's something else," I said. "The rock over by the satsumas. Was it there before?"

"Satsumas? Like little oranges?" Libby and Calvin looked at the bowl on the buffet. "We didn't have any satsumas."

Calvin picked up the rock and slid his fingers over the smooth surface. "I wonder what this symbol means? I wonder if it has significance?" he mused.

"I'm not positive, but I'm pretty sure it's Japanese kanji for 'energy.' I'll look it up tonight and let you know," I offered.

"I guess there's no point in calling the police, with the track record our neighbors have had," Calvin said. "On the other hand, I really think we should call them in the morning."

"The parade is in the morning, too. It will be crazy around here," Libby said.

"What parade? Rachel was talking about how excited she was for the parade, too, but I wasn't sure what she was talking about," I said.

"*Antiques Caravan*, that public television show, is rolling into town tomorrow. They're filming part of their opening sequence on Fourteenth Avenue to get some shots of historical houses in Seattle," Calvin said. "Rachel's extremely excited to be a firefighter on the sidewalk as the caravan passes by."

"It's not exactly a costume parade," Libby began, "but you know Rachel. Any excuse to dress up."

This was the first I'd heard about *Antiques Caravan* coming to town. It seemed it was news to Mom, too. Maybe everyone on the street had found out before we moved in.

Calvin walked Mom and me home, which Mom insisted

wasn't necessary. Calvin said he always made sure Rachel's babysitters made it safely home.

It was after midnight, but I needed to get some answers. I got out my list of things that had been changed in Libby and Calvin's house:

> Vase moved to family room
> Family photos moved to family room
> Dining room furniture rearranged
> Bowl of fresh fruit (satsumas) appeared
> Hot water container moved
> Polished stone with symbol for "energy" added

I pulled out *Feng Shui for Your Home* and began looking for any possible meaning. I wasn't sure if the bowl of fruit was significant because it was food or because of the orange color. I wasn't sure where to start, so I paged through the book, looking for meaningful words to jump out at me.

Family was the first word to get my full attention. In that section I found this:

"The Creativity and Children area is located in the West corner of your home."

Their family room was in the back of the house, facing downtown, the water, and the west. Apparently this was a good area for family photos and personal items.

Perhaps the dining room was rearranged because of

this philosophy: "You can change the flow of energy by moving your furniture around." The rock that said "energy" could be a token to remind us of the importance of energy and change. It was placed in the room where the flow of energy had been redirected.

Two things could explain the bowl of satsumas. Fruit represents abundance. I surmised that abundance in the dining room could represent a bountiful feast to keep the family healthy and nourished. I also read that the dining room should be the warmest room in the house, and one way you can warm it up is to introduce reds, golds, and oranges. The satsumas were doing double duty: as fruit they represented abundance; their orange color helped warm the room.

Much was written about electrical appliances. It was advised to not place water or a water source between an electrical outlet and an appliance. That could be why the toaster was moved to be right next to the outlet, and the water container was moved to remove interference.

It was one o'clock in the morning by the time I turned off the light. Luckily, the next day was Saturday, so I could sleep in.

CHAPTER 12

SO MUCH FOR sleeping in.

"Hannah, it's for you. It's Lily, and she doesn't sound happy," Mom said, handing me the phone.

"Hannah Jade West, I'm so disappointed that you didn't give me advance warning of the *Antiques Caravan* parade in front of your house," Lily started off, without even saying "Hello," "How was babysitting," or "So sorry to wake you up before noon."

"Huh?" was the only response I managed.

"My dad woke me up to show me the front page of the local news section. *Antiques Caravan* is doing a TV shoot on your street, as if you didn't know," she continued.

"Actually, I didn't know until—"

"I'm jumping in the shower now, and I should be there in a half hour. Maybe thirty-five minutes. I need to figure out what to wear," Lily said. "See you then."

I might as well get up and hit the shower, too.

Antiques Caravan is a superpopular show on public television. Once a week people tune in to watch other people find out if their family heirlooms are truly heirlooms . . . or just junk. It's pretty addictive to watch. Last week a man brought in an old map he'd found in his father's attic after his father died. The map was a 1928 Grizzly Gasoline Road Map of Montana. Just an ordinary map that you fold up and stick in your car's glove compartment. But this guy's dad had kept it neatly folded and stored in an envelope. The pristine condition, as well as the advertisement for a gas company that didn't exist anymore, made the map worth several hundred dollars. The man who now owned the map was ecstatic, even though he wasn't going to sell it right away.

That same week, a woman brought an ivory bowl that had been handed down through her family. She seemed confident that it was a true heirloom, worth a lot of money. Turns out it was simulated ivory instead of real ivory. In my opinion, that makes the bowl much more desirable. The thought of killing elephants for ivory is completely disgusting to me. Anyway, because it wasn't real ivory the bowl was valued at a few hundred dollars, not the thousands of dollars the owner had been expecting. Turns out that the map of Montana and the simulated ivory bowl were worth the same amount. One person was thrilled about it, the other sorely disappointed. Kind of funny how it all turned out. I'm sure there's a life lesson in there.

Each episode of *Antiques Caravan* opens with shots of the city they're visiting. They're called "establishing shots" because they establish the location with images of the city skyline and landmarks. They also try to show some local color. An old-style truck trailer with the *Antiques Caravan* logo leads a parade down a residential street in the old section of the city. I guess this time our street was the one they were going to use to showcase older homes in Seattle. This was the "parade" that Rachel had been so excited about.

What to wear for a parade? Let's see. How about jeans, high-tops, and my school ultimate Frisbee sweatshirt (the one that said "Chavez Ultimate"). Cool, but classic. I pulled the sweatshirt off soon after I'd put it on. I went to the closet and grabbed my mom's old Washington State University sweatshirt that had the cougar mascot's head on the front. It was vintage and cute—and added a certain local flavor to the *Caravan* crowd. Maybe it would earn me a second or two on TV.

I ran down the stairs when the front doorbell rang.

"I'll get it!" I called out to Mom. I swung the door open, ready to say something utterly witty and sarcastic to Lily, but when I opened the door I saw a firefighter. A little one.

"Hi, Hannah. Are you coming to the parade?" she asked.

"I hope this isn't too early to stop by," Rachel's mom said. "Rachel insisted that we make sure you were up and ready to go to the parade."

"Teenagers sleep too late on Saturdays," Rachel said.

"I'm up and I'm ready. I don't have a firefighter uniform,

so I decided to wear a cougar," I said. Rachel nodded, like she was giving me her approval, so I went on. "My friend Lily is coming over, too. Do you want to come in and have some hot chocolate and wait for her?"

Rachel nodded again and marched her little firefighter self into our house and toward the kitchen, calling for the cats as she went. "Jasmine! Sport! Simon! Reba! Dolly! Here kitties, kitties." She'd obviously spent time in the house and with the cats before.

Mom invited Libby in for tea, and the two of them went into the living room to talk. Rachel and I hung out at the kitchen bar counter on "the tallest stools" (as Rachel called them), sipping our cocoa and talking about different waving techniques for parades.

"I like this one," Rachel said, enthusiastically shaking her hand back and forth.

"How about this one?" I moved my left and right arms in an interpretation of a stop-motion animal.

Rachel giggled. "You look like a robot! Now I'm a princess, waving to my royal kingdom." My little fire-fighter friend did a quite impressive imitation of one of those beauty queens with fake smiles and tight, sparkly dresses who always appear on at least one float during a traditional parade.

"There's also this one," I said, extending my hand at a right angle and moving it in circles clockwise, then counterclockwise.

"Wax on, wax off," said Lily as she walked into the kitchen. We burst into giggle fits and continued "wax on, wax off," which is funny only if you've seen the original *Karate Kid* movie seventeen times like we have. When I try to explain why this is absolutely hysterical, I usually get a polite "Oh, that's nice" comment. This time, Rachel giggled along with us, caught up in our laughter.

"Love the outfit, Rach," Lily said approvingly. She looked at me, sort of smirked, and added, "Always so nice to see you, Hannah."

"Love your...boots" was all I could come up with in return. "I gather you're dressing in a historical fashion today?"

Lily was wearing a straight light brown linen skirt that reached midway down her calves. She had on dark brown tights and black leather ankle boots that laced up the front. A beige linen top was tucked in under a three-inch wide suede belt. A brown cardigan and her hair in a French braid were the final touches to her vintage look.

"The houses on this street are mostly circa 1901 to about 1915. I believe I've achieved a modicum of success dressing appropriately for that era," Lily said. Just then her cell phone rang, which kind of negated the historical authenticity of her getup. I mean, "outfit."

"Is it time?" Rachel asked, pointing to the clock above the stove.

"Yes, it is! Let's hit the streets," I said, helping her off the bar stool.

CHAPTER 13

"I GUESS THAT guy overslept," I said once we were outside. A man in his bathrobe was running down the street after what I presumed was his car, which, at that moment, was hooked up to a tow truck. The rest of the street was clear of parked cars.

The street looked wider and more majestic without cars parked next to the curb. The lack of cars really helped show off the towering oak and maple trees, while also opening up the view to show off people's front yards and houses.

The sidewalks were lined with people on both sides of the street. It looked like there was a good crowd along the parade route all the way down to Volunteer Park—about a five-block length. I recognized several people from the Block Watch meeting.

"If this had been just one week earlier, it would have been a parade to celebrate our moving in," I said.

"I'm glad you moved here," Rachel said, still clinging to my hand.

"Hannah, if you have time to let Rachel stay with you during the parade, I know she'd be thrilled. We'll consider it babysitting. Will that work for you?" Libby asked.

"Deal," I replied.

"I'll be nearby if you need anything," she said. "Oh, and here's a key in case you need to get into the house for anything," she added. I could tell she was relieved to be able to mingle with the neighbors on the sidewalk without constantly keeping an eye on a child. I've done lots of babysitting jobs where the mom or dad is in the house or in the yard, but just wanted a bit of a break. In fact, I had a couple of jobs as a "mother's helper" (even though it was really with a dad who ran a business out of his house, but no one says "father's helper") even before I took the babysitting class at Children's Hospital.

I looked around the small crowd, wondering if I'd see anyone from school. I saw the spiky-haired yin/yang woman, Louise, moving through the crowd, shaking hands and giving something to people. The younger woman with the apricot sweatshirt was there, too. She smiled as Louise introduced her to people. She looked across the street and waved to me and Rachel, too. I did one of those quick look-arounds to make sure she was waving to us before I waved back.

A white Ford F-something pickup (one of the really big kinds) was driving slowly down Fourteenth. A woman stood in the back talking into an amplified megaphone.

She was far enough away that I couldn't hear what she was saying. As the truck moved closer, I saw the familiar *Antiques Caravan* logo on the hood and the driver's-side door. The truck stopped in the middle of our block.

"Thank you for coming out on this glorious morning!" the woman's voice came out loud and clear, without any annoying buzzing or crackling. "We're so happy to be bringing *Antiques Caravan* to Seattle, Washington!" People began cheering.

"Thank you, thank you," she continued. "Now, let me tell you a little of what we're going to be doing. The first time the *Antiques Caravan*'s caravan," she paused for laughter, "will lead the parade heading north. A camera person will be walking alongside the sidewalk to capture your genuine excitement about the arrival of the caravan. Now that will be our first run-through. There will be at least one more. During the second one, the first vehicle you will see will be our camera truck, just an ordinary Ford pickup with cameras. The main camera will focus on the vehicles; two auxiliary cameras will, once again, capture your genuine excitement about the arrival of the caravan. And you will be genuinely excited, because the second time through our *Antiques Caravan* host Marcia Wellstone will be driving the truck, with cohost Bradford Hines in the passenger seat. We also have some guests from a local car club. Please relax and have fun! Thank you!"

As she talked, a man passed out a sheet of paper that

outlined basically what the megaphone woman had just said. It also showed the parade route. After our part, with "genuine excitement," was completed, the camera truck was going to continue into Volunteer Park to capture images of the water tower, the Seattle Asian Art Museum, and the Conservatory.

The truck moved to the next block and stopped in the middle. "The first time the *Antiques Caravan*'s caravan will lead the parade . . ." I could hear bits of the same speech we'd just heard.

"What's it say? What's it say? Can I have it?" Rachel asked, looking at the orange flyer I held.

"It shows where the cars and trucks are going to go during the parade and after the parade," I said. I turned it over. The backside listed the dates and procedures for trying to get an item appraised and featured on *Antiques Caravan*. Starting on Friday morning, people could bring their treasures to the Washington State Convention Center downtown. For two days, appraisers would screen the items. I handed the flyer to Rachel, who intently studied it as if imitating me when I read it.

"We totally have to be there on Saturday morning so we can get on the show. I think I have a good shot at getting selected," Lily said, smoothing the front of her linen skirt.

"Lily, it's not about you. It's about the items and their value. It's about whether your necklace or lamp or vase has a good story behind it," I pointed out.

"Nonsense. Personality and camera presence always come into play, not to mention clothing choices and a sense of style. Besides, I can make anything have a good story," she said.

An old-fashioned car horn *toot-tooted*.

"It's starting!" Rachel said, jumping up and down.

Indeed it was.

CHAPTER 14

MORE HORN HONKING. Friendly *toot-tooting*, not at all like the obnoxious horns on new cars and trucks.

We cheered and waved as the *Antiques Caravan* old-style panel truck came down the street. We kept waving for the camera. A black antique car followed. A sign on the door said "1914 Ford Model T." Underneath it said "Lake Washington Antique Car Club." Eleven more cars followed, all from the same car club.

One camera guy with a handheld camera came toward us to get a close up of firefighter Rachel. She tipped her fire hat, then reached over to give Izzie a big hug.

"Now that's a shot that's going to make it on TV," I whispered to Lily.

"Rightie-o," Lily said a bit loudly with one of her English accents. She succeeded in getting the camera guy's attention and he zoomed in on her, then backed away to get Rachel and Lily both in the shot. By default, I figured that my vintage cougar sweatshirt and I might also have a chance at being on TV.

"And yet another shot guaranteed to make it on TV," Lily said to me in her regular, nonaccented voice. She looked pretty smug about the whole thing.

"Hey, Chief," a college-aged guy with a clipboard said. "Just in case we use a picture on the show, we're going to need permission from your parents."

"I'm the babysitter," I said. "I'll get her mom over here."

"We may need one for both of you, too," he said.

"Of course!" Lily cooed, smiling warmly. "We've been through this before, haven't we, Hannah, dear?"

Luckily, I didn't need to be embarrassed because the clipboard guy had already moved on and hadn't paid any attention to Lily's pompousness.

The parade itself was pretty anticlimactic. It was over in five minutes. We'd have to wait at least ten minutes for the caravan to circle around and get back for the second run-through.

Rachel pulled my hand. "Hannah, I have to go. Now," she said.

"Can you hold it?" Lily asked. "The parade is going to start again soon."

"That's a little insensitive," I said, glaring at Lily. "She's only four," I mouthed.

"Now," Rachel said, tugging my entire arm with urgency.

"Okay. When you gotta go, you gotta go," I said to Rachel. "We'll be right back," I told Lily.

Rachel was moving a little slow for a kid who was

desperate to go to the bathroom.

"Let's hurry," I urged her. The unspoken part of that sentence was "before it's too late." Of course, Rachel has been potty trained for at least a year, but I learned in my babysitting class to take a child's request to go to the bathroom quite seriously.

"I'm okay," Rachel said.

"What? Don't you have to go?" I asked.

"Yeah, I do. But it's not an emergency or anything," she said. "I'm going to need help. You'll need to hold my fire chief hat and maybe my coat."

Apparently Rachel the Firefighter was planning ahead to avoid an emergency during the parade.

"Hi," I said, a bit surprised to see the young woman in the apricot hoodie coming down the driveway on the other side of Libby and Calvin's house.

"Oh, hello," the woman said. Neither of us said anything for a few seconds too long, which always makes me nervous and leads to my talking too much.

"I'm house-sitting at the Parkers'. But now I'm babysitting. You live on this street, right? Louise's neighbor? I'm Hannah, by the way," I said.

"I'm Rachel. I'm a fire chief," Rachel said, following my lead and introducing herself.

"I'm quite pleased to meet you, Chief," the woman said, holding out her hand for Rachel to shake. "My name is Georgia, and it's nice to know we have emergency staff here on such a busy day." She shook my hand, too, as I introduced myself.

"We're just running home to use the bathroom," I said.

Georgia looked at me, then realized I was waiting for her to say something. "Oh, right! I was just checking the iron. Ralph was afraid the iron was left on, and I volunteered to run over here and make sure it was turned off. It was. Off, that is. It was off. Ralph lives alone, and you know how things like that can be troubling. But all's well. I'll see you two back at the parade," she said.

Rachel giggled.

"What's so funny?" I asked. I was a little alarmed that the giggle might indicate we hadn't made it to the bathroom in time.

"She called Mrs. Rosetto 'Ralph.' That's silly!"

"Maybe Mr. Rosetto is Ralph?" I said, unlocking the front door to her house.

Rachel stopped laughing and looked at me very seriously. "There isn't a Mr. anymore. Mrs. Rosetto was really sad. Too sad to have trick-or-treaters. Now we won't have noisy ice cream at our picnic."

I speak Four-Year-Old, so this all made sense to me. Apparently Mr. Rosetto had died some time before Halloween. He must have brought homemade ice cream to a neighborhood picnic. He probably made it in one of those contraptions where you have to keep cranking it. Lily's dad did that, too. He was always trying to get us to help crank, but we didn't fall for that one anymore. It was a lot of effort for a little bit of ice cream. And Rachel was absolutely right: it was noisy ice cream.

Rachel handed me her hat as we ran down the hall to the bathroom.

"Emergency! Emergency! Coming through!" she screamed, adding a *wee-wooh, wee-wooh* sound like a fire truck. Once we took care of business, we headed back out to the parade. I'm always careful about locking the door when I leave a house, but this time I was hyperaware of being careful and making sure everything was locked.

"I need to take this to your mom so you can be on TV," I said, walking Rachel's permission form over to Libby. She and my mom were talking with Louise, the yin/yang woman, who smiled when she recognized me.

"This is my daughter, Hannah," Mom said, by way of introduction.

"We haven't formally met yet. I'm Louise Zirkowski," she said, extending her hand. I like it when grown-ups shake hands with me. "I live in the red house across the street. I believe you and I share an interest in tai chi tu."

I smiled, impressed that she said tai chi tu instead of yin/yang. Even more impressed that I knew what it meant. "I just met your friend Georgia at"—I didn't actually know whose house it was now—"at the Rosetto house?" I finished my sentence as a question. I hate it when I do that, but I really was questioning whose house Georgia had been at.

"Really?" Louise's forehead furrowed. "That's odd. Did you say Ruth Rosetto's house?"

"Yeah, she said she was just checking on something," I said. Ruth? Ralph? They sounded kind of the same. Maybe Rachel and I had heard Georgia wrong and she hadn't said Ralph after all.

Louise closed her eyes and appeared to be taking deep breaths. Then she opened her eyes. Her face looked relaxed again.

"Maggie, let me give you my card," Louise said, handing Mom a business card. "You may not need my services, but perhaps you know someone who does. I'm fairly new at it, but I believe I have quite a knack."

"May I have a card, too?" I asked. "I collect them."

"Of course!"

Louise Zirkowski handed me a card advertising her services. Below two familiar-looking symbols were the following words:

Louise Zirkowski

Feng Shui Specialist

CHAPTER 15

"FENG SHUI?" I asked, surprised by the coincidence.
"Are you familiar with it? You pronounced it correctly,"
Louise said appreciatively. I said it "fung schway." I knew
that wasn't absolutely positively correct, but it's as good as
most Americans can get.

"I've read a little bit. I don't know that much, but I like to
learn about Chinese traditions," I said.

"We should talk sometime, Hannah. In the meantime,
I should get back to the other side of the street. Our
instructions for today ask that we stay roughly close to the
same place in each take."

I showed the card to Lily, who seemed to register the
significance of the symbols right away.

"Can I hold it?" Rachel asked, apparently wanting to
hold the business card. I couldn't take my eyes off of it.
There was kanji above the words *feng shui*.

"Sure. I'd really appreciate your taking good care of it.
It would be really supercool of you if you let me have it
back when we go home," I said. Rachel nodded solemnly,

carefully holding the card and then putting it in her pocket.

"Here we go again," Lily said, pointing to the caravan.

A boring white pickup led the way, just as the megaphone woman had said. Next came the *Antiques Caravan* truck. I recognized the main host from the show, who was driving and waving. I recognized the man in the passenger seat, too, although I didn't know the names of either one today.

"Who are they?" Rachel asked, giddily jumping up and down and waving to the hosts.

"Marcia Wellstone and Bradford Hines," Lily said.

"Hi, Marcia," I called with the crowd.

"Hi, Marcia! Hi, Marcia!" Rachel followed my lead. Once again, the camera guy was right there to get a shot of Rachel. "Hi, Georgia! Hi, Georgia!" Rachel waved energetically to Louise and Georgia across the street. Louise nudged Georgia and pointed toward Rachel. A woman with a camera perched on her shoulder turned to get crowd shots across the street.

Louise smiled and waved for the camera just as her friend Georgia backed up and stepped behind a taller man.

Must not like TV for some reason. The exact opposite of my two companions, the fire chief and Miss 1906.

CHAPTER 16

"WELL, THAT WAS an exciting morning," Lily said when we got inside. She stopped in the entryway to unlace her boots and kick them off. She grabbed a duffel bag. "I'm going to change my clothes in your room."

Sometimes Lily may seem rude, but she's not. I like the way she doesn't need to ask for permission at our house (or wherever we're house-sitting), and I don't need to at her house. It's like each of us is part of the other's family. It's nice.

"While we're up there, let's think of something to bring to *Antiques Caravan,*" she said as we climbed the stairs.

"Good idea," I said. "It's too bad we have to go to school on Friday."

"I know. That means Saturday is our one and only chance to be featured on the show," Lily said.

"Featured?" I asked, raising one eyebrow (a trick that I'd just mastered). I headed out the bedroom and down to the art studio, with Lily right behind.

"Of course. A couple of young girls like us with a family

heirloom? Who could resist?"

I had put some of my own art supplies out with Happy's brushes and paints. I picked up my own brushes and took them out of the pot. "I know!" I exclaimed triumphantly. "This!" I held up my brush pot for Lily to examine.

"I love this pot!" she said. "It's so cool that your grandpa gave it to you. But I think we should come up with something showier."

"Nope. I'm bringing this." I had made up my mind. My mom's dad had died of cancer before Mom adopted me. But he had known that I was coming because Mom had been waiting eighteen months to adopt a daughter from China. He didn't really know about *me*, specifically. But he knew he would have a granddaughter someday. He had left a gift-wrapped box for my mom to open when she came back from China with me in her arms. Inside was a Chinese porcelain pot to hold calligraphy brushes (or, in my case, paintbrushes) and a small companion piece to rest a brush on. They were both robin's egg blue. The pot had a border at the top in green. Mom said it was as if her dad had predicted I'd be an artist.

"Hmmm . . . You do have kind of a good story there," Lily said. "I'm going to have to find something equally sentimental, but more valuable. I can't imagine that my parents have anything, but if they do, I'll find it."

After Lily left, I took out Louise Zirkowski's feng shui business card. It didn't take long to find the meaning of the characters. Next to the yin/yang symbol was the kanji for "tai chi tu." But this was Chinese kanji, slightly different than the Japanese kanji stones left in people's houses.

Feng shui is pretty popular. It was silly to think there was a link to the break-ins and Louise Zirkowski. Right?

CHAPTER 17

ON TUESDAY, Lily and I went to the Seattle Public Library downtown right after school. I love going to the library, especially the downtown one. It's an eleven-story building that has this weird shape on the outside and lots of glass everywhere. An architect named Rem Koolhaas designed it, a fact I like to throw in because it's fun to say his name. It's not what you expect of a library at all, yet it's full of books, so it immediately feels comfortable.

If I have enough time, I like to go to the reading room on the tenth floor. It feels kind of like a modem cathedral, basked in light. It's quiet and comfy.

Today we didn't have lots of time. We were on a mission. We headed to the Teen Center on the third floor and got on computers right next to each other.

"Oops, that's too many," Lily said. She had found hundreds of results in the online catalog when she typed in "antiques."

"Try something like 'antique guidebook,'" I suggested. Still too many books to look through. We wanted to find

some sort of guide that might give us a clue if our items
were worth enough money to actually get on *Antiques
Caravan*.

After we narrowed our search, we headed up the
escalator to the fifth floor.

"Can I help you?" a man asked. He probably assumed
we wanted a computer. There are more than one hundred
computers on that floor. But there's also a bunch of
reference books.

"We want to research values of antiques," I said.

The librarian took us to a shelf and pulled out three
books for us. "This is a good general place to start. We
have dozens more on the eighth floor, so if you're not
finding your item, we'll look up there, too," he said. "These
books have been very popular this week because *Antiques
Caravan* is in town."

"It figures," Lily muttered. "Everyone in Seattle is
probably trying to get on the show."

Everyone probably was. We'd preregistered online,
which gave us a number and a time to show up. Lily, me,
and our moms were going Saturday morning at ten.

I opened a book called *Kovels' Antiques & Collectibles*
and found the section on porcelain. It looked like my
brush pot and brush rest might be from the Ming Dynasty
(1368-1643). Of course, they could also be imitation. My
grandfather had left me several letters, and he never said
anything about the origins of the pot. They are beautiful

and precious to me no matter what. Still, it would be kind of cool to know how much they were worth. I wonder if that makes me ultramaterialistic.

"Wow! Let's find one of these!" Lily said. "Listen to this: jade and gold jewelry box estimated at *eighty thousand dollars*. Do you have one of these lying around?" She showed me the picture.

"Gosh, we don't have one just like that. Wait! Look at that vase," I said, pointing to another photograph. "That looks like the one Libby has. She said it was from her grandma."

We made a photocopy of that page to show Libby. I wanted an excuse to go to their house anyway. I needed to finish my drawing of Izzie on the corner of the couch.

We took the escalator down, stopping on the third floor and then the first floor. We stopped at the Teen Center for us, and then at the Children's Center to get picture books. I picked some to read to Rachel, and Lily grabbed a couple for The Brother.

Neither Lily nor I can leave a library without a book or two—or nine.

Mom made me wait until after dinner to call next door. As soon as Calvin heard my voice on the phone, he invited me over for cocoa. I asked if I might be able to draw Izzie some more and he said, "You bet. We'll make it a double cocoa."

I wasn't going to babysit, but I had a hunch Rachel would be disappointed that I wasn't bringing the Special

Day Suitcase. I grabbed a coloring book from the suitcase and a box of sixty-four crayons. I'd tell her it was a Special Art Day.

Mom walked me over. As soon as Calvin opened the door, I could smell the cocoa. It smelled delicious. It wasn't just ordinary instant cocoa: this was Mexican hot chocolate, my absolute favorite.

"Thanks! It smells so good, like the kind I get at Wired," I said, heading over to the counter and cradling a mug in both hands. I took in a good chocolatey whiff, just like I do at Wired Café where Mom works.

Mom laughed. "It *is* the kind you get at Wired."

Libby held up a canister of Wired Cocoa. "We love it. Thank you, Maggie."

"Well, you're welcome. But it was intended as a thank-you for helping us get this house-sitting job, not as Hannah's personal supply," Mom said.

Mom said good-bye, and Calvin promised to walk me home later. Then he turned to me.

"Can we see what you have so far?" Calvin asked, nodding toward my sketchbook.

I opened my sketchbook to show them, and then eagerly took another sip of my drink.

"Oh, Hannah, this is lovely," Libby said. "It conveys right away that Izzie is a part of our family."

Wow. That's exactly what I was trying to do. Cool.

"I'll help you re-create the pose," Calvin said. "Izzie, you lucky girl. You get some couch time." He patted the couch and Izzie obligingly hopped up, and then plopped into the corner.

"I moved the vase back to the dining room, but I decided those photos looked nice on the table here," Libby said. "I'll get the vase for you."

Rachel settled next to me and we began our Special Art Day projects.

"Calvin, could you come here a minute, please?" Libby said. My ears pricked up. Her voice sounded a bit tense.

"Are you sure you put it there?" Calvin said, speaking softly. "When was the last time you remember seeing it? Has the cleaning service been here? Are you sure it's gone?"

I couldn't resist. I put down my sketchbook and headed to the dining room.

"Is everything okay?" I asked.

"My vase. It's gone," Libby said, looking around as if it might suddenly appear.

A police siren broke the strained silence. Flashing red and blue lights pulsated through the dining room window. We all ran over and looked out, just as a second squad car pulled up. The officers jumped out and went to the house directly across the street.

CHAPTER 18

"WE'D BETTER STAY in here," Calvin said. "We don't know why the police were called. It might not be any of our business." Calvin, Libby, and I stood at the dining room windows, our eyes transfixed across the street.

I jumped when the doorbell rang. Calvin opened the door to let my mom in. I had a feeling she didn't like being in that big house all alone when something was happening across the street.

I jumped again when the phone rang. It was Grace, starting the Block Watch phone tree. Grace called Libby, and then Libby would call Louise, and Louise would call the couple next door, they'd call someone else, and so on.

"I need to call Louise, but let me tell you quickly. Someone broke into Mark and Tom's house. Their Chihuly bowl was stolen," Libby said. I'd never been inside Mark and Tom's house, but I know that Dale Chihuly is the best-known glass artist in the world. He lives in Seattle, but he's famous well beyond this city. A Chihuly bowl would be extremely expensive.

"Anything else missing?" I asked.

"Not that they've noticed so far," Libby said, dialing a phone number.

Calvin pulled out his cell phone. "I'm calling the police about the vase," he said. Libby nodded in agreement as she started talking with Louise.

"The dispatcher is sending one of the officers from across the street to talk with us," Calvin said.

"We don't need to stand here and watch those obnoxious lights. Let's all go back into the family room," Libby said.

Mom and I offered to stay for a while. We could help distract Rachel while Libby and Calvin talked with the police. Two officers came. One asked for permission to walk the exterior of the house to look for signs of entry. The other asked about the vase itself.

"Do you have a photograph of the vase?" the officer asked.

"No. Actually . . . Hannah, could you bring your sketchbook?"

It was already open to the drawing of Izzie with the vase. "Nice," said the officer. "Too bad it isn't in color."

I turned back several pages to the first drawing I'd done of the vase. I'd done that one with my Prismacolor pencils.

"That's perfect," Libby said. I offered to tear it out for them.

"Now, what can you tell me about the vase. Age, material, value?" the officer asked.

"I don't know much about it," Libby began. "It used to be in my grandmother's bedroom. I'd always loved it, so she gave it to me when I graduated from college. I'm afraid I don't know much more."

"I do," I said. I had completely forgotten to give Libby the photocopy from the book that showed a vase like hers. I pulled it out of the back left pocket of my jeans and unfolded it. I handed it to Libby, who passed it on to the officer.

"You certainly seem to have a keen interest in this vase," the officer said. She looked at me for few more seconds and then wrote something in her notebook.

I was about to tell the officer what else I had learned about the vase when I noticed her looking at me funny. Suddenly, I had a feeling that I had gone from being helpful to being a suspect.

Chapter 19

"There's certainly a lot to talk about at tonight's Block Watch meeting," Mom said during dinner the next night.

"Didn't they just have one? Geesh. How often do these people meet?" I complained because I knew that is what people expect from a twelve-year-old girl. But I already knew there was a regularly scheduled Block Watch meeting. In fact, I was eagerly anticipating it in case I could get any more clues about Libby's missing vase.

"Oh, stop," Mom said, clearly seeing through me. "You knew this meeting was scheduled. Didn't Libby already ask you to babysit?"

"Well, yeah. And I'm planning to stay close by again. I want to hear everything they discuss."

"I would expect nothing less of you," Mom said.

The meeting was at Calvin and Libby's again. We headed next door about fifteen minutes before the meeting started. I could start playing with Rachel and get her interested in some art project, and Mom could help Calvin and Libby put out trays of cookies and coffee.

Neighbors came in groups of two and more, opening the door and calling out "hello" as they did. Nice and friendly, but in my opinion things were a little too friendly considering that a series of thefts were happening on this street. Louise slipped in silently, mouthing "hello" to me and moving gracefully to sit on a cushion on the floor. I could picture her meditating in a similar position.

"This is great. We're all here tonight!" Grace began. "Thank you all for your cooperation during the *Antiques Caravan* parade. We have a lovely letter from the producers of the show, as well as some delicious Dilettante Chocolates, which I'll pass around for all to enjoy." Grace paused and looked around the room. "We have some tough topics to address tonight. Before we get to the theft at Mark and Tom's house, how about if we recap some of the odd things we've noticed in the past couple of weeks."

"I'm curious by what you all mean by 'odd,'" Louise said.

"'Odd' seems a bit mild," one man said. "It's a crime for someone to enter someone else's home. Sure, it's odd if things are rearranged, but the act of entering uninvited is well beyond odd."

"Did the rearranging appear to be an improvement?" Louise asked.

"Are you joking?" the man replied.

"Actually, dear, it did seem nicer when we came home," a woman said, patting her husband's hand as if to calm him down.

"That's not the point!"

"Clutter can create chaos and stagnant energy in our living spaces," Louise said, although I think most people—except me—had tuned her out.

"My house was tidier and my toilet bowl was closed. Remember?" Jodi said. "Tell me that wasn't odd." She said it in a breezy way, but I could tell she was still freaked out about the possibility of someone being in her house. As soon as she stopped talking she started biting her nails. I looked around at the Millionaire's Row dwellers to see what kind of nervous tics others might have. I could see the tension on people's faces. Everyone's except Louise's. She looked relaxed and content.

"It's worrisome to think of anyone being in your house or your private spaces," my mom said to the nail biter. I could tell Mom was trying to comfort her.

"How about if we hear from Mark and Tom," Grace said. She was a good leader. She stayed calm and kept the conversation moving. People seemed to respect her.

"I felt like something was off before I noticed that the Chihuly bowl was missing," Tom began.

"What do you mean by 'off'?" Calvin asked.

"I don't really know how to explain it. There seemed to be subtle changes, such as a chair moved at a slightly different angle."

"I hadn't moved anything, and neither had Tom," Mark said. "We called Geoffrey, our cleaning guy, but we didn't really think he had any insight into it because he hadn't been there for several days."

"What kind of changes?" Louise asked.

"Well, in the kitchen the coffeepot was moved so that it was closer to the sink," Tom began, but Louise interrupted.

"Was there anything between the sink and the coffeepot?" Louise asked anxiously.

"No. It was right next to the sink," Tom said, looking at Louise as if to say, Why are you asking such a completely weird, random thing?

Louise crinkled up her forehead as if something was worrying her. Why had she asked about the sink and the coffeepot? A mental image of Libby's kitchen counter popped into my head. That happens to me a lot: an image just pops into my head. Sometimes it takes me a while to figure out what it is I'm supposed to see in the image.

"Electrical can't be right next to a water source," Louise said softly, walking into the dining room. She wasn't talking to me. In fact, she wasn't talking to anyone, except maybe herself.

I pictured the sink in Libby's kitchen, and how the electric teakettle had been moved. My mind whizzed back to Happy's feng shui book and a paragraph I had read that said to place an object between a water source and an electrical source.

"Is the feng shui wrong?" I whispered to Louise.

She looked startled. "Yes. It's the opposite of feng shui. Very bad chi."

Did this mean that whoever was breaking into houses was anti-feng shui? (Or would that be un-feng shui?) Louise couldn't be the culprit. I could tell that she was so passionate about the art of placement that she would never do it incorrectly.

"Louise, we're going to make a comprehensive list of any strange occurrences. Could you come back into the living room?" Libby asked quietly. Louise nodded.

Calvin was taking notes on his laptop. "We have four separate break-ins and two missing items. Anything else missing? Have you noticed anything, Louise?"

"Missing?" Louise seemed to hesitate before she said no.

The grown-ups wrapped up their meeting, promising to keep in contact with one another and to keep an eye on all of their houses. Grace made sure that the cell phone and work phone numbers were all up to date. As people headed out, I maneuvered to be closer to Louise.

"Are you sure nothing is awry at your house?" I asked her. "You seemed a bit distracted earlier." I was impressed with my straightforward approach tonight.

"I may have misplaced something," she began. "I'm sure I'll find it soon. My son and grandson were here last week with their dog. It could have been moved. Or even broken by Ollie's wagging tail." I gathered that Ollie was their dog. Brilliant deductive reasoning, isn't it?

"I really am interested in learning more about feng shui. Right now I'm confused about why someone would break into a house to feng shui. You would never do something like that . . ." My voice trailed off because I wasn't really making a statement nor was I asking a direct question. Besides, I got sidetracked wondering if *feng shui* could be used as a verb.

"I don't break into people's houses!" Louise said. "That kind of intrusion would interfere with the chi."

She didn't exactly answer my question. Then again, I didn't exactly ask her the question.

CHAPTER 20

THERE WERE NO mysterious feng shui visits or burglaries on Millionaire's Row the rest of the week. That in itself seemed strange. Why the sudden stop? Did the thief think we were watching too closely? Mom was certainly watching me closely. If she's at work, I always call when I get safely home after school. This week, however, she insisted that I not only call when I first got to the front door, but that I keep talking to her the entire time I'm unlocking the door, going into the house, and turning off the alarm system. Happy and Frank's house was about the only house without an ACE Security sign—and also about the only house that actually had a working alarm system.

At long last, it was Saturday morning and time to head to the Convention Center for our chance to get one of our items appraised on *Antiques Caravan*.

Lily, me, and our moms carpooled downtown together. We could have easily taken the Metro. We even could have walked. But we needed the car because Mom was bringing a rather unwieldly object to the show.

I thought I would be embarrassed that my mom was carrying a lamp around, but we saw people hauling chests of drawers, cabinets, and other kinds of large furniture. There was a stash of grocery-style carts and flat carts for people to use.

The lamp belonged to Happy and Frank. They called to apologize for not telling us about the parade. When Mom said I was bringing something to the first-round appraisal, they asked if she thought it would be interesting to take something of theirs. I think what they were politely saying was that they had many valuable things in their house, and maybe we'd have a better chance to get on the show with one of their items. I thought for sure Mom would choose a piece of artwork, but here she was, carrying a table lamp.

"Lucky numbers 433, 434, and 435," Lily said. "I feel pretty good about those numbers." She was dressed, once again, in what she now called her "circa 1906 outfit." She had one addition to the outfit this time: a brooch that her mother had hidden away. The women in her family had handed it down to their daughters over the years. Lily's mom decided it was the right time to pass it on to her own daughter, making Lily the sixth to own it. "I never knew it was this old," Lily had told me earlier in the week on the phone. "I always thought it was just some dorky pin my mom wore on Thanksgiving and when we visit my grandparents." This morning Lily was wearing it proudly.

I counted about fifty-two people ahead of us. Our assigned time was eleven o'clock, with a suggested arrival time of ten o'clock.

"I read something that said that *Antiques Caravan* is an extremely popular show in prisons," I said. "Seems like pretty good thinking for those criminal minds. Gives them all kinds of ideas of what to steal when they get out."

"Why don't you girls go to Starbucks and get us some coffee?" Lily's mom said, handing Lily a twenty-dollar bill. Mom nodded, which surprised me. She likes to stay loyal to small coffee shops like Wired, where she works, and usually steers clear of big chains. But there was a Starbucks right in the Convention Center, so I guess convenience won out.

On our way back, I checked out the crowd, trying to guess who would make it on TV and who wouldn't. I was pretty sure Lily was doing the same thing. As I looked around, my eyes stopped on one particular individual. She wasn't wearing the same apricot sweatshirt this time, but I recognized Georgia, the Om Woman, right away. I pointed her out to Lily.

"That's Om Woman? I thought she'd look more zen and serene," Lily commented. She was right. Georgia was downright fidgety today. I thought she was alone, but then Louise joined her, handing her a cup of coffee. I hoped it was decaf, because Georgia was practically jumping from foot to foot. Like many others waiting for their shot on *Antiques Caravan*, they had a grocery cart for carrying their treasures.

We were lucky we didn't have to move any heavy objects. Mom was still hanging on to that lamp with one hand, holding her green tea with another. She raised the lamp a bit, which I realized was her attempt at a wave at Louise.

Louise bustled over.

"I didn't realize I'd see so many people I know here," Louise said.

"Isn't it amazing? Just think of all the treasures and interesting stories these people must have," Mom said.

"I suppose everything is a treasure if it has meaning to you. The problem is, people have so many things these days that they don't know what's important to them in life—or even in their belongings. Their acquisitive natures lead to all sorts of stress. They go shopping to buy things and then find themselves surrounded by chaos and stress because now they need to take care of all these *things*," Louise said.

"We are rather acquisitive, aren't we?" I added. I'm not exactly sure what that means, but it was fun to say it and sound smug.

"Yes, and less is always more," she said.

"I guess that's the feng shui way," I added.

"Just shui 'no' to clutter," Lily added. We all groaned a little at that one.

"I love your necklace," I said, admiring the yin/yang symbol that hung on a silver chain around Louise's neck.

There was a rumble of an announcement over the P.A. system. "I didn't quite catch what that announcement was, but I'd better get back to my friend Georgia and our place in line," Louise said. "As always, it's lovely to see friends and neighbors."

"You think she did it, don't you?" Lily whispered to me.

"What makes you think I think that?"

"You were doing that thing when you want to keep someone talking. 'We are rather acquisitive, aren't we?' Come on. That's not something you say every day. Or any day."

"Yeah, I do think she did it. It's the only thing that makes sense. Neighbors wouldn't think anything strange about seeing her out and about. It's weird that she would break into her friends' houses and handle their stuff, and then steal their stuff," I said.

"Hannah, it couldn't be Louise!" Mom said. I hadn't realized she was listening.

"But there's an obvious feng shui connection here," I said.

"Louise embraces many philosophies and beliefs, just like we all do. Just because she is studying feng shui doesn't mean she is presumptuous enough to feng shui someone's house without their knowledge. And I can't believe I'm using 'feng shui' as a verb," Mom said.

She might have said something after that, but I really couldn't hear her any longer. The sound inside the Convention Center was deafening. Hundreds of people talking all at once in a cavernous space that seemed to amplify sound. All four of the local TV stations had camera crews there ready to capture individuals' hopes and dreams for their items. I imagined that every station would start the story with images of the crowds and long lines, and then they'd talk about how many people were there and how long we waited in line. People watching at home would probably feel a little sorry for us because most of us would spend so much time only to find our items were worthless, at least in terms of monetary value.

Mom lifted her lamp-holding arm again, this time waving to her friend Mary Perez from KOMO TV. Mary waved back, imitating Mom's lamp-lifting gesture. I was definitely going to watch the news tonight. Mary is the kind of reporter who will find the most interesting story of the day. Two of her most interesting stories featured our first two big cases in Belltown and on Portage Bay. Yep. Mary always did the best stories.

Our instructions said to stay in line until the first-round appraisal crew came by to get some general information and take a quick photo. The first-round appraiser we got didn't seem to be enjoying his job very much.

"Name? Number? Object?" He wrote down just the basics and then took a picture with a digital camera.

"That's it? My future will be decided by that guy?" Lily whined.

I'd read up on how the show worked, so I wasn't as worried. "They're going to send the digital image to an appraiser who specializes in a particular area. If the item looks intriguing to that appraiser, our number will be posted on the big digital screen over there."

"But he just had me hold the brooch in my hand. He didn't get a picture of me," Lily whined. I knew she was kidding. She's a drama queen to be sure, but she's not conceited or unreasonable.

We found a place to sit down and eat our lunches. I looked around for Georgia and Louise, but I didn't see them. I certainly didn't see Georgia before I practically ran into her, head to head, on the way to the bathroom.

"Hi, Georgia," I said. "I don't know if you remember me. My name is Hannah. I live across the street from Louise," I said. Look at me! Friendly girl with grown-up manners!

"Oh, hey, I thought you looked familiar. Nice to see you again. My name's Georgia. Wait. You already knew that. My last name is Smith. Georgia Smith. Hey, would you be willing to watch my box while I go into the bathroom? I can't figure out any way to keep Louise's and my things safe and take care of business, if you know what I mean."

Georgia eased the box onto the floor. I said I was happy

to keep an eye on things. I'd be even happier if I knew what kinds of "things" I was watching (but I didn't actually say that part). I bent over to look inside, but all I could see was a bunch of bubble wrap and tissue paper. I poked around a bit, but everything was wrapped tight. I was tempted to try to unwrap the items a bit, but it was too risky.

"Thanks so much," Georgia said when she came back out.

"No problem," I said. "What did you bring here today?" I asked. I sounded exactly like Marcia Wellstone, host of *Antiques Caravan.*

"Me? Oh, just a . . . bowl. A salad bowl. My uncle found it at a Goodwill somewhere in Michigan," she said.

A bowl, eh?

"What kind of bowl? Ceramic? Glass?" I inquired. I was really thinking: a Chihuly bowl? But that was crazy. A blown-glass bowl by Dale Chihuly was certainly not an antique.

"Ceramic. What about you? Did you bring something? Or are you here with your parents?"

"I brought a Ming Dynasty brush pot my grandfather gave me," I said, realizing, of course, that it could be imitation. "My mom is here, too. She's hauling some old lamp around. She also brought a ton of food, so come find us if you want to eat."

"Right. I'll do that. Thanks again for keeping an eye on

my . . . bowl," she said as she lifted the box and walked away.

"Good-bye," she called over her shoulder. I stood as if rooted to the carpet. I could wait a few seconds and head in the same direction, following her. I wanted to know what was in the box.

Unfortunately, I had something else I needed to take care of first. At that moment I needed to go to the bathroom.

CHAPTER 21

"I TOLD YOU those numbers were lucky!" Lily squealed as the digital board showed that numbers 433, 434, and 435 were to go on to the next stage.

The guy who had checked us in told us where to go if our numbers were posted.

"It looks like we need to go to three different areas," Mom said. "How do you girls want to do this?"

"I can go alone," I said. I held up my cell phone, in anticipation of Mom's question, which would most certainly be "Do you have your cell phone?" followed by "Is your cell phone fully charged?" Yes, and yes again.

"Okay, *call me* if it seems they're going to continue with your pot, and I'll run right over," Mom said.

I headed over to a section labeled "Asian Art."

"I'll need your release, signed by someone over eighteen, like a parent, and your registration form," a girl said at the entrance to the section. I handed her my paperwork, completed and signed by my mom, and she checked me off a list.

"Hello, what's your name?"

I was surprised to see that Marcia Wellstone, the main host of *Antiques Caravan*, was speaking to me. I remembered I'd seen her talking about Chinese art and artifacts on the show before. This must be her area of expertise, on top of being the main host. Suddenly everything lit up, and I knew the cameras were rolling. Man, once they start moving on this they really move fast. There wasn't any time to call Mom.

"I'm Hannah," I said.

"It's wonderful to meet you here in Seattle, Hannah," Marcia said. "What do you have here today?"

I held out my hands with the brush pot and brush rest.

"Let's put them on the table here. What can you tell me about these pieces?"

I wondered if I'd perhaps lost the ability to talk, now that there was a chance this might be on TV. Lily and I had been on a TV show called *Dockside Blues* last summer, but no matter how important Lily tries to make it sound, we were still just extras. I'd never actually had to talk.

"This is a porcelain Chinese brush pot that my grandfather gave me. It was designed to hold calligraphy brushes. And this coordinating piece is where one would rest his or her brush when taking a break." Whoa! Look at me! I rattled that off like some sort of expert. I felt as if I were outside my body watching as someone else took over.

"Both pieces are quite lovely, aren't they? And it seems that they were indeed intended as a set. Do you know anything about the age or the style?" Marcia asked.

Here I go again: "I think this style of pottery is from the Ming Dynasty, which would mean it was made somewhere between 1368 and 1643. I don't actually know if it's real. It could be an imitation of something from the Ming Dynasty."

"Your knowledge is quite impressive," Marcia said. She smiled. She seemed nice, and all of a sudden I felt completely relaxed. "Did your grandfather tell you all of this?"

"No, actually I went to the library and looked it up in *Kovels'*," I said.

"That would be *Kovels' Antiques and Collectibles*, an excellent resource," she said. I could tell she was clarifying my source in case we really ended up on TV. The title of the book would probably appear on screen, too. "Hannah, your research at the library has certainly paid off. These pieces are, in fact, from the Ming Dynasty. The color at the top tells me that these were created in the later part of that dynasty, probably between 1612 and 1624."

I saw that my mom had come into our section. Maybe she had a hunch that the bright lights meant they'd chosen me.

"Is your grandfather of Chinese descent?" Marcia asked.

"No, he wasn't. He's my mom's dad," I said, pointing to Mom.

"Great! Let's get Hannah's mom in this story," Marcia said. They exchanged quick handshakes and introductions.

"So these items were a gift from your father?" Marcia prompted Mom.

"Yes. He bought them for Hannah before she was born. He died several months before I actually went to China to bring her home. But my dad knew she was coming, and he knew she would be a much-loved girl," Mom said. Uh-oh. She was choking up. This always happened when she talked about her dad and how he died before he met me.

"He left me a note that said he knew I'd find my way in the world artistically," I said, to divert some attention from Mom, in case she completely blubbered.

"That's a lovely story. Do you use these items?"

"I do use them. I'm an artist, just like my grandfather predicted," I said.

"Excellent. Well, Hannah and Maggie, these items are authentic, but they are not rare. The value for the brush pot is $545, and $230 for the brush rest. Are you going to hang on to them?" Marcia asked.

"Absolutely. I'm keeping these forever," I said.

"I'm sure you'll make good use of them and take good care of them. Thank you so much for sharing your story with *Antiques Caravan*."

The lights turned off. Instantly things felt dark and cold. I've been around TV cameras and lights enough to know that it always feels that way once the harsh, bright lights go away.

"That really was great. Thank you so much!" Marcia said. "I really enjoyed this segment. We'll let you know when it will air."

CHAPTER 22

"DID YOU HEAR that?" I asked Mom when the crew had moved on to someone else. "She didn't say *if* the segment airs, she said she'll let us know *when* it will air. As if it's a done thing!"

"You were great!" Lily rushed up to me.

"You saw it?" I asked.

"Yeah, we have some time to kill before they get to us," Lily said.

"How about you, Mom? What's up with the lamp?"

"Who cares? I'm just so thrilled about your fame," she said.

"Does that mean they weren't interested in the lamp?" I asked "You've been hauling it around for nothing?"

"I'll have you know that they were quite interested in the lamp. The first round estimate is that it's worth more than $4,000. But I don't have any emotional attachment to this lamp, and I have a bit of an attachment to you. I'm sure Happy and Frank don't mind. They probably know exactly how much the lamp is worth anyway," Mom said.

"Maybe that's exactly how much they paid for it," Lily said.

"Anyway, I'm glad I gave up my spot," Mom said. She gave me a big hug.

Her devotion to me also meant she'd be lugging that lamp around for the rest of the day.

The TV lights were back on in our section.

"Let's watch this next one," Mom whispered.

"It's Louise!" I hadn't realized she was in the same section I was. Marcia Wellstone had already gone through the introductions before we got close enough to clearly see and hear everything.

"I understand you're quite knowledgeable about feng shui, the Chinese practice of placement and arrangement of space, which is believed to achieve harmony with the environment," Marcia said.

"I'm studying feng shui, and I make it a part of my daily life in my work and living spaces. But I believe it will be a lifelong study. There is so much to learn," Louise said. "It is a discrete system involving a mix of geographical, philosophical, mathematical, aesthetic, and astrological ideas. Feng means 'wind,' and shui translates to 'water.'"

"Are there a few basics you could give us now?" Marcia prompted.

"It's quite complex, and Americans tend to make light of it. But in general, color dictates much of what happens in a room. Red is a creative, energetic color and is best used on a southern wall. If you have a creative job, you might consider a red southern wall in your work space. If you work at home, you should make sure the toilet lid stays closed, especially if it's in a straight line from an outside exit. Otherwise money that comes into your home might be flushed away."

Mom put her hand on my arm as if to keep me from jumping up and down while pointing and screaming "Ah-ha! *You* are the culprit!"—which is exactly what I wanted to do. I knew it all along, and I wanted to make that known, too. Well, almost all along. Now the two specific examples Louise gave were exactly what she had done to houses on Millionaire's Row. Okay. She hadn't exactly painted a wall red, but there were those paint chips taped up to a southern wall in one of those big brick houses. Closing the toilet lid in Jodi and Charlie's house had deprived their animals of an extra water source, but Louise thought it was important for them to have it closed.

"Anything that applies to *Antiques Caravan*?" Marcia asked Louise.

"Definitely. You should know the history of the objects in your home. If a piece of furniture or an artifact was stolen or was once owned by someone who went bankrupt or otherwise met bad fortune, you may want to reconsider having that item in your home," Louise said.

"Let's talk about the item you brought from your home," Marcia said. "What can you tell us?"

I hadn't paid much attention to the bowl that was on the table next to Louise. She picked it up and I still couldn't tell what was significant about it. It looked a little like a bowl I made for Mother's Day in fourth grade. It was unglazed terra cotta with a zigzag design painted or etched on the perimeter.

"From what I've been told, this is early Chinese painted pottery, possibly as old as 2000 B.C. It's hand modeled, and the walls appear to be built by cording. As you can see, it's only about six inches in diameter and so was probably used in the home for food or beverage," she explained.

"Looks like you can have my job," Marcia said with a laugh. "You're absolutely right. This is a Neolithic pottery bowl, Majiayao Yangshao Culture, from the Machang phase, which places it somewhere between 2000 and 2300 B.C., although I have a hunch it's closer to the 2000 B.C. mark, which, of course, is quite impressive. The condition is good. There are a few minor chips to the rim, but they're quite minor and don't detract from the significance of this rare piece. May I ask how you came to have this?"

I was grinding my teeth. She probably stole it from one of our neighbors.

"It was a gift from my ex-husband," Louise said. She seemed to catch something in Marcia's face. Louise laughed and quickly added, "My ex-husband and I remain dear friends, and I don't believe there's any negative energy associated with how this piece came into my possession."

A likely story, I thought.

"Any idea of the value?" Marcia asked. Louise shook her head no.

When Marcia gave the estimated value, there was a gasp from the crowd. It was definitely an amount worth gasping over. Staggering. I can't even repeat it because it blows my mind.

And to think Louise had probably stolen it from the rightful owners.

The TV lights turned off and several people rushed to speak with Louise and Marcia. Maybe she'd sell it before she left the building.

CHAPTER 23

MOM WAS KEEPING a tight leash on me, so to speak, trying to keep me from getting involved in Louise's—or whoever it rightfully belonged to—bowl.

"Louise seems so happy right now. Maybe we can just leave her alone for a while," Mom said. "Besides, she said her former husband gave her the bowl. She obviously knows quite a bit about its history."

I wasn't convinced.

If I couldn't get to the truth today, I knew it would come out when *Antiques Caravan* aired. Or maybe this part wouldn't air. I'd read that the *Caravan* research team thoroughly researched each item before it was featured on the TV program. When the show first started years ago, they'd featured a painting that had been stolen from a private collector eighty years ago. The painting had fallen off the radar of those in the art-appraising world because the crime had happened so many years ago. But the much-loved painting was part of one family's history, and the great-grandniece of the owner recognized it on the air. Ever since, *Antiques Caravan* had scrupulously researched each item mentioned or even shown in passing.

That was all reassuring, but it sure would be a lot more fun if I exposed Louise and her crime today.

Still, I went along with Mom and hoped I'd convinced her that I was being mellow about all this. We wandered around for another ninety minutes, waiting for Lily's brooch to be appraised. We eavesdropped on other people's appraisals and even talked to people about their treasures.

"Let's look in here. I love Art Nouveau," Mom said.

Georgia was standing behind a table. There were two objects on the table. One was a red glass bowl. The other was a blue vase.

Libby's blue vase.

"That's . . ." I started to say to Mom, but a guy with a headset on called out, "Quiet on the set." The lights came up, focused on Georgia. "Five, four," the guy with the headset was counting down, "three, two, one . . ."

"You have two quite distinct items here, so I've asked my colleague to join me," a man in a bow tie said. "Let's start with this vase. What can you tell us about this vase?"

"I don't actually know that much. My grandfather gave it to me. He died before I was born. He left it, along with a note, with my mother to give to me," she said. Hey, wait a minute! That's my story. Had she seen my segment and decided to use my story as her own? That would make sense, since she couldn't have her own story because the vase wasn't hers.

"You have no idea of the age or its origins?" bow-tie man asked.

"No . . ." she stammered. Origins? I'll tell you the origins! I scrawled a note to Mom: LIBBY'S VASE!!!!

Mom scrawled, "Sure?"

"Absolutely," I wrote, and underlined it three times.

Bow-tie man was talking about Art Nouveau something or other. Mom motioned that she was going to go make a phone call. I hoped she was calling the police.

"It's value is $3,200," bow-tie man finished. "But what we really want to talk with you about today is this magnificent iridescent piece of Louis Comfort Tiffany glass."

There was a gasp behind me. The camera guy and the sound woman glared at me. Hey, it wasn't me! I turned around to face Louise. Her eyes were huge, her eyebrows raised, and her hand clasped over her mouth as if to keep herself from screaming.

Ah-ha! *You* are the culprit! I wanted to say it out loud, but I knew I couldn't. I mean, I could say it out loud, but I didn't want to get in trouble with those TV folks. I just didn't have the guts to do it. If only Lily was here. She'd seize this opportunity to be on national television and catch a culprit.

Clearly, Louise and Georgia had been working together. Clearly, Louise had no idea that Georgia was going to come on *Antiques Caravan* with items the two had stolen in their feng shui scam. I wasn't sure who owned that Tiffany glass piece, but it was undoubtedly someone on Millionaire's Row.

"Tiffany? Really?" Georgia said.

"You seem surprised. What can you tell us about this bowl?"

"It's . . . it's also from my grandfather. It's quite old," Georgia said.

"I'd say this is from about 1910. Our culture today often hears about Tiffany glass lamps. Reproductions of the jewel-toned lamps are everywhere," the man said. "In fact, the reproductions can be rather inexpensive."

Georgia nodded.

"An authentic Tiffany lamp could be several thousand dollars," he said. "Excuse me, I meant to say a Louis Tiffany lamp could be worth several *hundred* thousand dollars. A Magnolia floor lamp has been valued at $1.5 million."

"Really?" Georgia stammered with excitement.

"Indeed." He held the bowl up to the light. "This is Favrile, a type of glass process patented by Tiffany in 1880. Different colors of glass are mixed together while hot. Vases and bowls may not be as valuable as the lamps . . ." The man paused.

"Really?" Georgia said again, the disappointment clear in her voice.

"A vase could range from $60,000 or more . . . ," he began, but Georgia interrupted him.

"Really!"

"Yes, as I was saying, ranging from $60,000 to $80,000 on the high end, and a couple of thousand dollars on the low end."

I waited for Georgia to say "really" again. She said nothing. She looked like she was holding her breath, waiting for the verdict.

"Many of these pieces are unmarked. Tiffany pieces have been handed down in families, and people haven't even realized what they had. Did your family know?"

"We had no idea," Georgia said. "We always took special care of it, but that's just because it seemed fragile. And beautiful. It's obviously beautifully crafted."

"Indeed. Beautifully crafted. Many bowls like this were crafted around 1902, but few survived, possibly because people didn't realize they were Tiffany. I'd value this piece at $22,000 to $24,000."

"Oh, my!" Georgia said, her face flushing. "My grandmother, I mean grandfather, would be so excited!"

"So would my aunt," Louise practically hissed from behind us. "Although Aunt Betty always knew that bowl was Tiffany."

"You mean it's yours?" I asked incredulously.

Louise nodded. "Absolutely. That little thieving . . . thief!"

"But aren't . . . aren't you . . . ?" Now I was the one faltering.

"The feng shui culprit? Yes. The thief? No."

And I believed her.

CHAPTER 24

"WILL YOU ENTERTAIN offers for this exquisite Tiffany Studios bowl, or do you intend to keep it in the family?" the appraiser asked.

Georgia was beaming. "I'm definitely open to any offers."

I'll just bet she is.

"Quick! Your phone!" I said to Mom, holding out my hand. Only my mom wasn't back.

Louise handed me hers. Excellent. It was a camera phone. I maneuvered my way through the crowd so I could get photographs of Libby's vase and Louise's bowl. I was too far away to photograph it really well, but I gave it a shot anyway.

"Come on!" I motioned to Louise. She stood in the back of the crowd, frozen. As I turned back to Georgia, two security guards came and escorted her away. People in black polo shirts with the *Antiques Caravan* logo whisked in to protect the fragile—and valuable—items.

"Louise, let's follow them," I urged her.

"I wonder if I should just let it go," she said softly. "It's all my fault after all."

"It's not your fault if she stole something from you. Did you see that blue vase she had? I'm sure that was Libby's vase. And I bet Mark and Tom's Chihuly bowl is in that box of hers somewhere, if not on her dining room table," I said. Louise looked years older and inches smaller to me. She looked sad to the core.

"Louise, I should apologize to you. I thought you were the feng shui thief. I was sure it was you breaking into houses and trying to make the energy flow better through feng shui," I said.

"I thought I was helping them," she said softly. "I had no idea people would see it as an intrusion. I thought they'd welcome the improvements in their living spaces and what that can bring to their lives. Georgia was studying with me. I thought she was helping me. But . . ."

Mom came back just then.

"What did the police say?" I asked Mom. "Do we need to stall Georgia? Tail her?"

"I didn't call the police. I would have sounded like a crackpot. I called Libby, hoping she would call the police with the case number. But I didn't reach her."

"Maybe we should bring Louise and go backstage to see if we can confront Georgia now," I said.

"Louise? Is she still here?" Mom asked.

I looked around and realized that she wasn't.

She had probably taken off when she heard the word *police*.

CHAPTER 25

MOM AND I looked around for Louise. We didn't see her. Georgia and her entourage of *Antiques Caravan* staff people had disappeared, too. The security guards probably thought they were keeping the bowl safe from thieves. That was kind of a twisted joke.

"We made it on TV!" Lily squealed, coming up behind us. "I wish you could have seen it. We were magnificent."

"Lily, we don't have absolute confirmation that they're using us," her mom said. She was beaming, too. There was so much energy buzzing around this whole *Antiques Caravan* setup. It would be impossible not to get caught up in it. And who doesn't love the idea of being on television?

"Who are you looking for?" Lily asked. "Hoping for another shot of fame today?"

But I didn't have time to explain. "Excuse me," I said to an official-looking person with a clipboard and the standard black *Antiques Caravan* T-shirt. "Do you know where we could find Ms. Smith? She was the one who was just here with that glass bowl," I asked the member of the crew.

"I believe she went back to our office area to entertain offers on her Tiffany piece, or, as you say, that glass bowl," he replied.

"We'd like to make an offer," my mom said. Yay, Mom! The man looked her up and down, as if deciding she had expensive enough shoes to be able to make an offer to Ms. Smith. Mom purposefully moved the lamp to a different position. She'd been lugging that thing around all day and now it was finally paying off. She held it confidently, as if she'd just purchased it from someone. If you can buy a $4,000 lamp—an ugly $4,000 lamp—on the spur of the moment, maybe you can buy something ten times that much, too.

"Yes, then, come with me." We all started following him. He stopped abruptly and turned. "Just two of you, please."

Obviously that would be Mom and me. Lily stepped forward, but I elbowed her back. "I'll go, Mom. I'll help carry my new bedside lamp," I said, trying to sound like a sweet but spoiled rich kid.

The office area was nothing fancy. Not at all. There were card tables and stacks of paper, boxes of files, computers with a zillion wires tangled together.

"Please write your offer on this form," the man said. "Ms. Smith will evaluate all offers in a few minutes. We'll be taping her again as she looks at the offers. It's a new segment for the show."

I grabbed the form from Mom.

"Manners, Hannah!" she scolded.

"My apologies. I assure you I can take care of this for you, Ms. West," I said formally.

Instead of writing a dollar amount, I wrote, "Hi, Georgia! Did you know my neighbor Libby has a vase exactly like that blue one? Only thing is, hers was stolen. So was Louise's red Tiffany bowl." I signed it, "Love, Hannah," which I thought was a nice friendly touch.

The camera crew came in. A makeup person powdered Georgia's nose and put a microphone on the collar of her shirt. Georgia smoothed her hair and quickly put on lipstick. They positioned both the vase and the bowl next to her.

"Now, as you examine the offers, please feel free to tell us as much or as little as you'd like," Marcia Wellstone coached Georgia.

Georgia began opening envelopes and pulling out each form. She looked extremely serious as she read the first one, then smiled and said, "This is a *very* good offer." She smoothed the form and put it to her right. She opened the second one and, again, looked at it intently. "A good offer, but a bit lower." She put it to the left. Envelope three brought "Another *very* good offer" and earned a place in the pile on the right. Envelope four went to the left; envelope five to the right. She spent more time on the form in envelope six. No smiles this time. She looked around anxiously until she spotted me. I waved. It was a friendly wave. After all, I'd signed the note "Love, Hannah."

Our envelope didn't make it into either pile. Georgia tossed it aside and in one swift move she scooped up Libby's blue vase and Louise's Tiffany bowl. No time for bubble wrap to protect the items. No time to comment on the contents of our note. Georgia bolted out of the makeshift office and into the halls of the Convention Center.

Mom and I followed her out, winding our way through a maze of office chairs and boxes.

"There!" I said, pointing to Georgia once we were out on the Convention Center floor.

"Watch it! Please!" a man snapped at us. Just in time, too. I'd almost plowed into the carved wood bench he and another man were carrying.

"Sorry!" I said, dodging to the right to keep moving.

"Slow down!" a woman said. She pushed a cart with a wingback chair.

This time I dodged to the left.

"This way!" Lily said. "She came cruising right by us. Let's go!"

We didn't find her.

Libby's vase was gone. Louise's bowl was gone.

Worse, now Louise and Georgia were gone, too.

CHAPTER 26

IT WAS PRETTY anticlimactic to come home after that crazy day. No TV cameras in the kitchen waiting to interview us. No thieves in the hallways for us to track. Mom had called and left messages for Libby and for Louise. She refused to let me call the police directly until we had talked with our neighbors.

Libby didn't have a chance to call us back until late afternoon. We told her everything and then brought our photos over to her house. She was looking for the case number to reference for when she called the police again.

"I don't know how seriously they'll take me," she said. "There must be all kinds of people who claim that something they saw on *Antiques Caravan* is really theirs and was stolen."

But this was different. Libby had reported it stolen *before* it appeared on *Antiques Caravan.*

"You really should call the police right away," Calvin said. As if on cue, Rachel brought the phone to her mom.

Turns out the police saw it my way this time. Sort of.

They agreed that because the vase had been reported stolen *before* I saw it at the TV taping, it was worth looking into. Two things I hadn't expected: They didn't exactly trust my claim that it was absolutely the same vase (even when I told them I had photographic evidence) and, worst of all, they wondered why a kid like me had such interest in a stolen vase in the first place.

"You seem to have quite a bit of interest in this vessel," an officer said to me. Mom and I stayed at Libby's house until the police came. Lily and her mom had gone home, but with a sincere offer to vouch for my astute eye for details.

"I know. It's weird, isn't it?" I said, hoping that agreeing with police officers made me seem like a cooperative witness, rather than a possible culprit. "I sketched it a couple of times when I was babysitting Rachel. That's why I know it so well."

I offered my sketchbook to the closest officer.

As she looked at it, Rachel brought me a crayon drawing she'd done of the blue vase, too.

"This is excellent," I said, giving her a hug.

"I also have photos of the same vase at the *Antiques Caravan*," I said. "Oh, wait. I don't." I forgot that I borrowed Louise's camera phone to snap a couple images of Georgia with the vase and the bowl.

"Photos of the little glass doodad you mentioned would be helpful," one of the officers said.

"Actually, it's a bit more than a glass doodad. It's a 1910 Louis Tiffany glass bowl," I said.

"Once again, you seem to know quite a lot about these valuable items."

"Yes," I answered. What else could I say? Maybe this officer thought I was suspicious, but at least I'm always honest.

"Excuse me, I just heard a knock at our front door," Libby said. A few seconds later she was back.

"Officers, this is our neighbor Louise Zirkowski, the owner of the missing red bowl," Libby said as Louise came into the room.

"Are you ready to report this item as stolen?" one officer asked. She nodded. They handed her forms. She, in turn, handed them a file folder with several pieces of paper in it.

"I've photocopied my family's bill of sale for the bowl. It's dated 1903. There are also photographs of the piece as well as a description from when we had it insured," she said. "I also want to give you this." She handed them one more piece of paper. "This is the information on Georgia Smith. She was an apprentice with me, studying feng shui. We believe she has the items."

I smiled at Louise to show my support. I was also trying to be supportive so she'd tell a little more.

"And . . ." I prompted. Still nothing. "And wasn't there

something more about feng shui you said you were going to tell us all?"

"Yes, I suppose there is. Thank you, Hannah, for keeping me on the right track. Officers, you may have information on another case from Fourteenth Avenue East. Some of my neighbors reported someone coming into—breaking into—their homes and . . . rearranging things. In some cases, things were tidied up. In other cases, items were left, such as a bowl of satsumas." Louise looked pointedly at the bowl of satsumas on Libby's dining room table.

The officers didn't look too interested in this discussion. It was pretty clear that the neighbors at the Block Watch meeting had been right. The police had never taken the complaints that seriously to begin with.

"The thing is . . . I'm the culprit in that one," Louise said.

I couldn't believe she said "culprit"! All those times I'd looked at her and thought: Ah-ha! You are the culprit!

"You're the one who broke into homes?" one officer said. She looked skeptical. Perhaps she thought Louise was covering for someone else.

"Oh, no! I didn't break anything, or break *into* anything," Louise said. "I have keys to most of the houses on the street. I often water plants and feed cats when people are away. We're a friendly neighborhood."

"Did the neighbors know you were going to use the key at times they hadn't specified? I assume you have keys to check on plants while they're on vacation, take in the mail, that sort of thing. That's quite different from entering in the middle of the day and messing up someone's belongings."

"Messing up? I wasn't messing anything up. I was just instilling some feng shui principles into their living spaces," Louise said. She sounded humble, and even a little bit ashamed.

"I believe that still constitutes breaking and entering," one officer said. He looked at the other, as if waiting for her agreement. She nodded. "We'll get back to you on that. I'm not sure what charges we'll press. In the meantime, it looks like we need to track down one Georgia Smith."

"You might be able to catch her at the Yogini Center. She told me earlier she was planning on going to the four o'clock vinyasa class," Louise said.

The officers looked at her and shook their heads before leaving the house.

"Louise, I don't understand how you think that you were doing people a favor," Libby said gently.

"I don't think that anymore," she said. Then she let out a deep sigh. "I thought people would know right away that it was me. I've been talking nonstop about feng shui, and I left those calming stones as gifts, and as a sort of calling card. But Hannah here made me realize that what I'd done was a bit . . . creepy, to say the least." She smiled at me. I, of course, had to smile back. Because once again a twelve-year-old had set a clueless adult straight.

The phone rang, and Calvin raced Rachel to answer it.

They came back into the dining room, with Rachel riding on her dad's shoulders.

"All taken care of," Rachel said. "The police say a-okay."

We looked at Calvin for an interpretation. "That was the police. They picked up Georgia. They met her as she was coming out of her yoga class. She was carrying a yoga mat, and a box with a vase and one glass bowl. Another glass bowl—a more modern blown-glass one—was found in the backseat of her car. Sounds like it's Mark and Tom's missing Chihuly bowl."

CHAPTER 27

You're invited to a special screening of

Antiques Caravan

Starring **Hannah West**
and **Lily Shannon**

Friday at seven o'clock in the evening

at Libby and Calvin Greenfield's house

Showtime begins promptly at eight p.m.

BYOD

(Bring Your Own Dog)

YOU CAN'T SAY the word *party* around a four-year-old unless you fully intend to follow through. When Libby and Calvin mentioned they wanted to have a party the night that *Antiques Caravan* aired, Rachel immediately started talking party plans.

Libby insisted that Mom and I invite whoever we wanted. Mom had agreed, but only on the condition that Libby let her help out with the hostessing duties. Once that was agreed to, Mom and I realized that it would be a nice way to bring together the people whom we had met during our different house-sitting gigs.

As we went over the guest list with Libby, Rachel had begged for stories about each person. She especially wanted stories about their dogs. She particularly liked the story about Ruff, the cairn terrier who had played a part in my first case.

"I want to meet Ruff," Rachel announced. "Can we invite Ruff?" she asked her parents.

Calvin hesitated, but Libby rushed in with a yes.

"We don't have to invite Ruff," I said gently to Rachel. "We have all the dog we need right here with Izzie."

"Izzie wants to invite Ruff! Izzie wants all the dogs to come!" Rachel said. "Can they, Mommy? Can the dogs come?"

This time Libby hesitated. "I guess so," she said.

"Yippee!" Rachel said.

Calvin gave Libby one of those "What have you got us into?" looks. Mom often sent that same kind of look my way.

"Is Louise coming?" Libby asked Mom on the night of

the party. They were in the kitchen slicing tomatoes and chopping basil.

"She said she'd rather not," Mom said. "Something about how she's taking a break from using electronic devices."

"Maybe the whole ordeal is still painful for her," Libby said.

"Maybe she didn't think she should come without a dog of her own," Lily said.

The doorbell rang, and things got a little crazy as the party guests and their dogs arrived. Dorothy Powers and her cairn terrier, Ruff, were the first to arrive. Mom and I met Dorothy when we were house-sitting in the Belltown Towers.

Mango, a labradoodle we'd taken care of on a houseboat last summer, arrived with his owner, Jake Heard, and his neighbor, Alice Campbell. Elvis, a basset hound, made his entrance, dragging his owner, Piper Christensen, behind him. We'd taken care of Elvis in Fremont. Not far behind Elvis was Scooter, a big shaggy dog from Fremont, with his owner, Benito.

"Dad couldn't come," Benito said. "He's on a case. By the way, he said to tell you congrats on your big case." Ben's dad is a private detective. I felt proud that someone like Tom Campo recognized my sleuthing skills.

"Maybe Hannah can give your dad some tips," Lily offered.

"Hannah, so nice to see you!" Ben's grandfather, Mack

Pappas, shook my hand. He took off the old-fashioned hat he almost always wore and placed it on the table in the entryway.

Mom's friend Nina came with another artist, James, and their friend Polly Summers. The last guest to arrive was Jordan Walsh. I had gotten to know Jordan during our first case. I hadn't expected that we'd end up as friends, but it just worked out that way. Now we have Japanese and art together, and we're partners on a project on artists for our U.S. history class. Jordan, Lily, and I even eat lunch together every day at school.

Mom was in her waitress mode, making sure everyone had snacks and drinks. Calvin made sure everyone had a comfortable place to sit where they could see the TV. That second part wasn't really a problem, since the TV was so huge.

"It's going to start! It's going to start! *Wee-wooh, wee-wooh!*" Rachel was wearing her fire chief outfit again. Her fire-engine imitation made everyone laugh, but they quieted down as the theme music for *Antiques Caravan* started. The camera scanned the Seattle skyline as the music faded.

"There I am!" Rachel squealed. She somehow picked her tiny little red fire chief hat out of the throng of people along the sidewalk as the lead *Antiques Caravan* truck came down Fourteenth Avenue.

"There I am again!" Rachel squealed. "Look at me! I'm

here, and I'm there!" She stood next to the TV, pointing to herself in her fire chief outfit, and then pointing to herself onscreen in her fire chief outfit. "I'm double! I'm twins!"

"We'd love to have two of you," her dad said.

The next close-up was of Lily in her circa 1906 outfit. I was right next to her, proudly wearing my cougar sweatshirt. "Grr!" Rachel said, giggling and pointing at me.

The TV showed the houses along Millionaire's Row, each one looking more stunning than the last, and then showed some highlights from Volunteer Park and the Seattle skyline at sunset.

I was the second person featured on the show. And let me tell you, it's really awful to watch yourself on TV. I don't sound the way I think I sound in real life.

"This is a porcelain Chinese brush pot that my grandfather gave me. It was designed to hold calligraphy brushes. And this coordinating piece is where one would rest his or her brush when taking a break," I said to Marcia Wellstone. I glanced over at Mom. She was beaming with pride. I looked back at the TV. I guess I looked okay. The red streaks in my hair looked good on air. And I was wearing my beloved long-sleeved yin/yang shirt, a step up from an ordinary T-shirt or my cougar sweatshirt.

"I hope I'm not too late for the party," Mary Perez, Mom's friend, entered the family room.

"You missed seeing the incredibly interesting me," I said. "Your loss."

"Believe me, Hannah, I saw you many times. I have this show practically memorized. You were all spectacular," she said. Mary did a big story for KOMO TV on the stolen items that showed up at the *Antiques Caravan* taping. The story was so juicy it had been picked up by the network and aired on national news. A part of the story would be part of tonight's show, too.

"And now, ladies and gentlemen . . ." Lily said, as the show moved to the jewelry segment.

"It's you!" Lily's brother, Zach, exclaimed. "You're dressed funny."

Lily shushed him. They weren't on long, but I have to admit that Lily was pretty relaxed and good on camera. She might be right about this acting thing.

Marcia Wellstone and Bradford Hines were in an elegant wood-panel office for the next segment.

"Something highly unusual happened when we were in Seattle," Marcia began.

"Yes, indeed, Marcia," Bradford Hines agreed. "As our viewers know, we thoroughly research each item that makes the final cut to be featured on our show. We don't want there to be any errors, nor should a piece be featured that has a questionable history."

The camera showed a close-up of Louise's bowl as Bradford Hines described the significance of Tiffany glass. The host also described Libby's blue vase, and showed it from several angles. Libby looked over at the vase on the table, as if to make sure it was right where it belonged.

"In an odd turn of events, it appears that both of these items were stolen from homes on Seattle's Millionaire's Row, the same street you saw at the beginning of tonight's program. Thanks to the work of Hannah West, the young woman we featured earlier with the Ming Dynasty brush pot, who also happens to live on Millionaire's Row, we were able to put all the pieces together. We asked reporter Mary Perez of Seattle to bring you the full details of the story."

We all watched as Mary went over the facts of the story. She interviewed Mom and me on camera about our involvement. Mom explained how we were professional house-sitters and so it's part of our job to look after our clients' belongings. Mom added that it often extended to looking after the neighbors' homes and well-being, too.

"Hannah's photography and sketching skills have figured into a few other incidents here in Seattle in the past year. Perhaps the police department should hire this seventh-grade artist permanently. From Seattle, this is Mary Perez."

"*You* are all over TV!" Lily said. She didn't sound jealous at all, and I knew she wasn't.

"I guess this is my fifteen minutes of fame?" I asked. No one answered. Everyone was talking at once.

Rachel handed me a new drawing.

"It's you and your mom and Vincent and Pollock," she said. "It's your family."

"I love it!" I said. And I meant it. In the drawing, my two goldfish were the same size as Mom's and my heads. Somehow, that seemed just perfect.

"I really like it here, but I hope people don't end up thinking that we actually live on Millionaire's Row," I whispered to Mom. "It totally blows my image as a struggling artist."

"Well, no matter what people think, I'll always be proud of you," Mom said, embracing me.

"Thanks," I said, hugging her back.

I looked around the room and was amazed to see so many people I knew in one place. I tried to stop all the corny thoughts percolating in my head. But these weren't just thoughts. They were feelings. And they were coming from my heart.

Suddenly, it didn't seem to matter at all that we didn't have a permanent address. Being surrounded by family and friends felt good. It felt like home.

Q and A

with NANCY PEARL

and LINDA JOHNS

NANCY PEARL: Where did the inspiration for the Hannah West books come from?

LINDA JOHNS: My favorite mysteries are stories set in real places, like *Harriet the Spy*, which takes place in New York City. My favorite city is Seattle, where I've lived most of my life. I wanted to write a mystery story that was set in Seattle, but it didn't all start coming together until I had the character of Hannah West in my head.

I needed a way for Hannah to be in different parts of the city so she could solve mysteries. I knew she also needed some sort of "cover," a way to be out and about observing things. A good detective is always observing. Walking a dog is a great way to explore new neighborhoods, and it seemed natural that Hannah, a dog lover, would have a dog-sitting and dog-walking business. If Hannah and her mom were also professional house sitters, they'd have a chance to live in fancy places and meet all kinds of interesting people. And all of this gave me the opportunity to spend countless hours walking my dog, Owen, around funky and charming neighborhoods.

NP: Why did you choose to make Hannah Chinese?

LJ: I based the character of Hannah on one of my favorite girls, who happens to have been born in China and adopted by an American family. I hadn't read many books for young readers that represented the people I know and see every day. And I didn't know of any books, at that time, with a main character who was Chinese-born and adopted as a baby and brought to the US.

NP: When you wrote the first book, *Hannah West in the Belltown Towers*, did you think you'd write three more about the same character? Do you ever think about writing more about Hannah and her friend Lily?

LJ: I'm very attached to Hannah as a character and I hoped that I'd be able to write more stories starring Hannah solving mysteries. I wrote and rewrote the first mystery several times, with lots of edits and tweaks in each new version, before I sent it to my agent. I wrote a brief overview about two more potential mysteries. I was thrilled to get to write not just two, but three more. I am sure there are more mysteries that need to be solved in Seattle, and I think Hannah and her best friend Lily are the duo to do it.

NP: When did you know you wanted to be a writer? Did you write stories as a child? If so, do you still have some of them? How do you feel reading them now?

LJ: I was in second grade when I decided I wanted to be a writer. My mom kept the story that set me on this path. It was really sweet of her to keep it, and it was also indicative of how much both my parents supported me as a writer. In fact, every job I took as an adult, my mom would always ask, "Are you sure you'll have enough time to keep writing?" But back to my second grade story: It would have been better with more action. It still delights me to remember how much fun I had writing it.

NP: Do you like to read? What sorts of books? As a child, were you a big reader? How did (or not) your parents encourage you to read? What were some of your favorite books as a kid?

LJ: I love to read! Right now I tend to read mysteries and general fiction. I read books written for children, teens, and adults. I'm from a family of readers, and it was a common occurrence to see my parents and my sister and I all together in the living room, each a world away in a book. We were definitely a family that took "reading together" to heart. My parents encouraged me to read whatever caught my fancy. Sometimes that meant sitting next to a set of encyclopedias and flipping through the pages. The "D" encyclopedia was my favorite because it was the one with several pages on dog breeds and their history.

At my elementary school, once we were in fourth grade, our daily reading time was spent in the library reading whatever we wanted. How great is that? Almost an entire hour each day at school where you could sprawl out on the floor or curl up in a chair and read. I claimed the "H" aisle in the library as my reading spot because that's where Marguerite Henry (she wrote horse books, like *Misty of Chincoteague*) was. I read my way through the library, choosing a book from each section. Whenever we finished a book, we'd sit down with our librarian, Ms. Elrod, and talk to her about what happened in the book and what we liked about it. A lot of who I am now is grounded in those hours in the library and the conversations with Ms. Elrod.

When I was younger, I loved the picture book *Harry the Dirty Dog* by Gene Zion, illustrated by Margaret Bloy Graham. My friend Hannah (who is a librarian) gave me a Harry the Dirty Dog T-shirt for a recent birthday and I am so happy whenever I wear it.

NP: If someone liked your books, what others would you recommend?

LJ: Try the Gilda Joyce mystery series by Jennifer Allison. Gilda is a psychic investigator who often underestimates how her own intelligence is what's actually solving a mystery. She's a resourceful spy and has a flair for disguises when she needs to go undercover. And don't miss *The Wig in the Window* by Kristen Kittscher, starring best friends Sophie Young and Grace Yang as unstoppable young detectives. *The Westing Game* by Ellen Raskin is an older mystery (published in 1978) that I think stands the test of time. It features a young detective piecing together clues to solve a rock-solid mystery. *The Westing Game* is my all-time favorite mystery, and that includes the adult mysteries I've read as well.

NP: I know that you're a librarian—is that a good career choice for someone who likes to read and write stories?

LJ: Being a librarian is a perfect job for someone who loves reading and writing! In addition to getting to be around books and talk about books, a librarian spends a lot of time working directly with people and hearing their stories. A big part of being a writer (or a detective!) is observing people and tracking down information. A librarian gets to do this every day, a hundred times each day.

I had a great professor at the University of Washington who inspired many of my coworkers and I to be librarians. Her name was Nancy Pearl and she taught us that there is a book for every reader. If you can get someone to talk about a book he or she has loved, you can pick up clues to find the right book at the right moment for that reader. Writers, detectives, and librarians—we all use clues, stories, and information to save the day.

ABOUT the AUTHOR

LINDA JOHNS is a writer, reader, and librarian. The order changes depending on the day. She works at the Seattle Public Library's downtown Central Library, a gorgeous eleven-story building with a million books inside. She grew up in Cheney, Washington, and graduated from Washington State University with a degree in journalism. She has a master's degree in library and information science from the University of Washington. Her first job, at age fifteen, involved a lot of stapling. Subsequent jobs (after college) included reporter, editor, and bookseller. Linda lives in Seattle with her husband, son, and a basset hound named Owen Henderson.